Torey's Prayer

Tracey V. Bateman

Heartsong Presents

To Angie Shivers.
Glory to God, who heard your prayer.
And to Torey Shivers, His merciful answer.

Chapter 11 is dedicated to my niece, Tiana,
who never lets me forget that ONE pumpkin pie...smile

A note from the Author:
I love to hear from my readers! You may correspond with me by writing:

> **Tracey V. Bateman**
> **Author Relations**
> **PO Box 719**
> **Uhrichsville, OH 44683**

ISBN 1-59310-115-5

TOREY'S PRAYER

Our mission is to publish and distribute inspirational products offering exceptional value and biblical encouragement to the masses.

All Scripture quotations are taken from the King James Version of the Bible.

prologue

Chicago 1906

Where is he?

Torey peeked through the heavy, gold-colored curtain and gave a not-so-ladylike stomp. The least a man could do when he escorted a person to the theatre was to be in the booth when the curtain went down for the last time. She'd been sitting alone for the last half hour, and she simply couldn't tolerate one more second.

Irritation rose and strengthened her resolve. No matter that her stepfather had told her to stay put, she was going to find him before the theatre shut down and she was left all alone.

She swept aside the curtain and stepped out before she could change her mind.

During her trek down the hallway, her too-small slippers bit into her heels. She winced, limped, and tried to endure, until finally she could bear it no longer. Halting, she rested her hand against the wall behind the curtained booths and slipped off the painful shoes. She pressed them together in one hand and hid them in the folds of her skirt. Relief flooded her as her stocking feet sank into the threads of the red carpet.

She wandered down the deserted hall, hoping to catch sight of her stepfather. Just as she was about to give up and return to her booth, she heard a voice and stopped short.

"I tell you, I cannot extend you another loan. I apologize if this inconveniences you, Amos. But perhaps you would be better served to work harder to pay off your debts than to spend your days playing the horses."

At the sound of her stepfather's name, Torey's ears perked up, and she stepped closer to the booth. She drew the curtain aside enough to peek through without being seen herself.

"I need that money." The threatening tone in Amos's voice sent waves of dread through Torey's stomach. It was a tone with which she was well acquainted. "Otherwise, I'm ruined."

Ruined? What of the vast fortune Mother had left when she died? Surely Amos hadn't squandered it all away in less than three years.

The other man appeared to have no sympathy, evidenced by his hard-edged tone. "You should have thought of that before borrowing all over town and then spending the investment money on a horse."

"H—how could you possibly know that?"

Torey had never seen Amos so weak. The sight sent a shiver of revulsion down her spine.

"Let's just say our mutual acquaintances have warned me about you. Now, if you'll excuse me, my son surely must have ordered the carriage around by now. He is likely wondering as to my delay."

"Please, you're my last hope."

"I'm afraid there is nothing I can do, even if that were my inclination." The gruffness of his tone had softened, and Torey could hear the compassion in the man's voice. "The bank has a certain set of standards. I'm sure you understand. There are protocols I must adhere to."

"You're the president. You can do whatever you choose." Amos's voice dropped in pitch but carried chilling intensity. Torey shuddered.

"Yes, but I don't own the bank. I merely oversee it for someone else."

"But surely you are able to—"

"I'm sorry. Do you read your Bible, Mr. Williams?"

"What has that got to do with this?"

"The Word is full of sound financial advice as well as spiritual lessons. I encourage you to see to your spiritual condition. God can help you in every area of your life. Even where you fall short with money. But it really is your choice."

"I humble myself and beg you for help, and you offer me religion?" Anger boiled in Amos's voice. "I'm ruined!" He paced from one end of the booth to the other.

"I apologize if my advice offends you. But advice is all I can offer. Now, I really must go."

Amos spun on his heel, his face twisted with rage. "You really must go nowhere."

The gleam of light on a steel blade registered in Torey's mind. She opened her mouth to scream, but her throat remained clamped shut, allowing no sound. Then it was too late. Amos's arm came down swiftly, and the man slumped.

From deep within her, a groan made its way to Torey's lips. Amos turned abruptly, the knife clattering to the floor at his feet. In a split second, he reached the curtain, grabbed her arm, and pulled her inside the booth. "What were you doing, eavesdropping?" he demanded, his fingers biting into her arm.

"I—I was looking for you. Th—the opera is over." She looked at the gray-haired man lying on the floor, a red stain spreading across his white shirt. Tears filled her eyes. "Why, Amos?"

His brows narrowed. "That's my business. If you know what's good for you, you'll forget what you saw." He dropped his hold on her arm and busied himself going through the man's pockets like a common thief. "You're an accessory now."

"A—a what?"

"Accessory. That means you helped commit the crime."

"But I—I didn't!"

A sneer marred his otherwise handsome face. "If you tell

the police you saw the whole thing and didn't warn this poor man, they'll consider you as guilty as I. If you keep your mouth shut, they'll think he was murdered by someone bent on stealing." He showed her the money, then shoved it into his coat pocket and tossed the man's wallet on the floor.

"But you *killed* him." Torey's voice rose to a shrill.

"Shut up, you little idiot!" He clamped his large hand over her mouth and hissed against her ear. "Now, you be a good girl and act as though nothing has happened. Understand?"

Torey nodded, fear licking her insides like a forest fire.

"That's better. Let's get out of here."

Amos removed his hand from her mouth and grabbed her once more around her upper arm. He pushed back the curtain, letting his gaze drift down one side of the hall and back. Apparently satisfied that no one was going to notice him leaving the booth, he stepped out, dragging her with him.

When they reached the top of the stairs, Amos leaned close to her. "Get that look off your face."

"I–I'm sorry, Amos. But your fingers are hurting my arm. I can't help it."

With an impatient sigh, he released her. The sudden movement caused Torey to stumble and knock against a man who had just ascended the steps and now stood with them on the landing.

"Careful," he said. His hands went to her arms to steady her.

Curiosity mingled with amusement flashed in the gray eyes staring back at her.

"I beg your pardon," she murmured. Embarrassed, she averted her gaze.

"Did you lose something?"

"Excuse me?" She cut her eyes upward.

Reaching down, he retrieved one of her slippers from the top step.

With a trembling hand, Torey accepted it. "Thank you, Sir."

Amos stepped forward. "Yes, thank you. I apologize for my daughter. She is rather eccentric. Always taking off her shoes at the most inopportune moments."

"Eccentric, you say?" The man's brow rose. Torey couldn't tell by his voice if he was amused or repulsed, but neither assessment of her by this man necessarily made her feel better.

"Quite," Amos replied.

"Well. . ." The stranger cleared his throat. "I must be going now. Good evening to you both."

Shame burned Torey's cheeks. Not that she would ever see the man again, but did Amos have to make her appear as though she belonged in an insane asylum?

"What did you think you were doing?" Amos demanded. "We haven't the time for your flirtations." Torey bit back a cry as he snatched her arm once more.

They had just reached the bottom of the stairs when an anguished scream echoed through the building. "Father!"

"Don't turn around," Amos warned. He opened the exit door.

At the sudden commotion behind them, Amos tightened his grip on her arm.

"Someone—please! My father's been murdered!"

Torey yanked away and turned. At the top of the steps stood the same man who had given her back her slippers. Horror filled her and bile rose to her throat. She looked at Amos.

He sneered. "Don't speak a word, or I will kill you too."

The evil radiating from him terrified her. Looking into his dark eyes, which flashed their hatred and warning, Torey knew. . .he was going to kill her anyway.

She couldn't resist the sudden tears.

"Where is a porter?" Amos groused.

"All the employees have run inside to help, I believe, " Torey said, very near to hysteria.

"Come on. We'll have to get the carriage ourselves."

To the back of the theatre? There would be no lights, no one to see if Amos tried to kill her. At best, she would be in his clutches forever. He'd make sure she didn't tell anyone what he'd done. Her future loomed before her in her mind, and she shuddered.

Strong survival instincts made their presence known. "No!" she yelled. She jerked free and ran for all she was worth.

one

At the *clip-clop, clip-clop* of horse's hooves coming down the cobblestone street, Torey Mitchell ducked under the cover of a large, nearby oak. Trembling, she watched the carriage pass, then resumed her slow gait along the sidewalk, breathing a sigh of relief to be in a section of town where thugs and thieves weren't lurking behind every corner building.

Two weeks. It had been two weeks since she had seen the murder. And she'd been roaming the streets of Chicago ever since—snatching moments of sleep in filthy, deserted alleys. Stealing food from outdoor vendors when she could get away with it. Exhaustion tapped every muscle in her body. And hunger had become a constant, malevolent companion.

Torey knew she couldn't wander like this indefinitely, but where could she go? Amos Williams knew every businessman in town, including the seedy ones—especially the seedy ones, it would seem. Already she'd been recognized as his step-daughter at least a dozen times. She'd always known him to be a harsh man. She'd always tried her best to keep her distance from him, fearing the cruelty she'd witnessed him display to the servants. But never, never in her wildest imaginings had she considered him capable of murdering a man in cold blood. He deserved prison. And she was the only person in the world who could bring about justice for his victim. But every time she saw a police officer on the street, her heart beat with a fear like nothing she'd ever experienced. The thought of going to prison or being hung was too much to bear.

At other times when she was feeling her most brave, she wondered if perhaps the police would understand that she'd been too terrified, too horrified, to scream for help. It wasn't that she hadn't wanted to warn the poor man.

Regret haunted her over her choices that night. If only she had not gone looking for Amos after the opera. She should have stayed put in their booth until he returned—as he'd instructed. Never would she forget the flash of his knife, the look of startled fear in the victim's eyes, or the dark anger in Amos's face when he heard her gasp and turned to see her watching in terror.

Now she couldn't go home.

Nor could she ask assistance from friends and acquaintances. Who would believe her word over Amos's?

If Amos put out the word that she wasn't to be helped—and Torey was almost certain that he had—no one would dare hire her. Not that she was qualified to do anything anyway. She'd watched her own maids work enough to know their routine. The problem lay in the fact that she'd never actually made a bed or cleaned a water closet. The thought of domestic work didn't exactly excite her, but right now she'd do just about anything for a slice of bread, an apple, anything to quell the ache in the pit of her stomach.

She sighed with longing at the soft glow of lamplight shining from the stately homes with well-tended lawns. She averted her gaze from the windows, not wanting to intrude on the families just sitting down to dinner.

As she returned her attention to the sidewalk, a gray squirrel scampered across the path. She stifled a scream and instinctively jumped back. A wave of dizziness washed over her, and she swayed. In a split second of clarity, she reached out, grabbing a wrought-iron fence just in time to prevent herself from plunging to the ground. She leaned her head against the railing and closed her eyes. For just a moment she would stay here. Only long enough to get her bearings, then she'd be on her way. Maybe she could find a nearby park with a soft, grassy surface where she could sit and stretch her aching legs.

Once the world righted itself again, Torey dared to open her eyes. As she prepared to move ahead, her gaze caught the open window of the house behind the wrought-iron bars.

Bathed in lamplight, a woman knelt before a wingback chair, her elbows resting on the cushioned seat, her head bowed in prayer. From somewhere deep within Torey, a sense of longing—stronger than her need for food—rushed up like a swelling tide. Mother had never been the religious sort, and the thought of Amos darkening the doors of a church was nothing short of laughable.

But Torey remembered a gray-haired woman who had walked the floors in prayer. How she missed her grandmother! Grandmother had filled her early childhood with love, laughter, and God. If only she could have stayed a child forever. Tears pricked her eyes.

On impulse, she fingered the latch on the gate. Did she dare sneak up the walk for a closer look?

The woman wiped away a tear, and Torey moved almost before her mind informed her of the decision to do so. She closed the gate carefully behind her, wincing as it groaned in protest. Once she was certain no one had heard the groan and was coming to investigate, Torey crept stealthily to the window, veering from the stone walk to catch the best view. The woman's tears continued to flow as her lips moved in prayer.

"Our Father which art in heaven," Torey began to recite, pulling the words from the recesses of her memory. "Hallowed be Thy name."

She whispered every line, marveling that she remembered the words to the prayer. And before she said *amen*, her heart poured forth words of entreaty. "God in heaven. Jesus? I haven't heard Your name spoken in anything besides a curse for many years, but if You are there, as Grandmother always promised You would be, I beg of You, please help me."

"What do you think you're doing?"

Amos!

Fear sprang up inside of Torey. Terror.

Rough hands seized her, biting into her already bruised flesh. Suddenly face-to-face with a stranger, relief that it wasn't Amos warred with fear of what was to come from this man who had caught her peeking through the window. "Answer me, Girl. What were you doing lurking about in the dark?"

"I–I. . ." Torey's world began to spin "Please, I'm. . ." Her mind registered his gray eyes widen in surprise. Worry washed the anger from his countenance just as she drifted into unconsciousness.

≈

Simon reached out just in time to grab the waif of a girl before she fainted dead away on his doorstep. She hung like a rag doll in his arms and he stood, looking about in helpless wonder. What did one do with an unconscious thief?

He glanced down. Long lashes brushed her dirt-smudged cheeks, and for the life of him, Simon couldn't look away from the lovely, almost angelic face framed in golden curls.

The door swung open. Simon jumped and glanced up quickly, as though he were a thief caught with stolen merchandise.

"Mercy, Simon, a person could have mistaken you for a gypsy. I very nearly phoned the police."

"I'm sorry for frightening you, Mother."

Mother's eyes narrowed. "Who is this?"

"As a matter of fact, it appears we have a thief, though I doubt she's a gypsy. I caught her peeking in the window at you. How many times have I told you to be sure and draw the curtains at sundown when I'm not home?"

Mother's plump hand touched the brooch at her throat as it always did when she was nervous. "To think someone could just look in on a person without her knowledge. Did you knock her out, Simon?"

Expelling an exasperated breath, Simon gave his mother a wry grin. "I haven't sunk so low as to strike a woman, Mother. She fainted when I confronted her."

"Woman? She's hardly more than a child. And of course she fainted. You must have scared her half to death." His mother shook her head. "Well, bring her on inside and let's get her settled into Georgia's old room."

"You want me to bring her inside the house?" Simon asked incredulously. "Do you think that's wise?"

"Of course. It is our responsibility to see her cared for, considering you caused her to faint."

"Mother, this is not our fault. Nor do we bear any blame for this waif's condition. She was lurking behind a bush, up to no good, I'd venture to say."

"Nonsense. Look at her. No one with the looks of an angel could be up to no good. Now, obey me, please. Or do you prefer standing in our yard arguing with your mother while the neighbors observe our humiliation?"

Simon scowled and glanced about.

His mother chuckled. "There *might* have been an observer."

A grin sprang to his lips. She had a way of getting her point across quite nicely. He carried the girl up the stairs and into the house. "Are you sure you want me to put her in Georgia's room?"

"A lovely girl should sleep in a lovely room. Your sister hasn't occupied that room in five years. I'm sure she won't mind."

"I know. I was just thinking the extra servant's quarters might be better." The girl was filthy.

"Don't be snobbish, Simon dear. Take her upstairs to Georgia's room as I requested. I'll follow as soon as I draw her a bath."

"All right. But under protest."

"Duly noted."

Simon deposited the girl on his sister's rose-colored comforter, then closed the door softly after him. The smell of roast beef filled the house, tempting his taste buds and beckoning him down the steps toward the source of the tantalizing aroma. He waited impatiently in the kitchen while Mother tended their new guest.

In moments, she appeared.

"Poor girl. I decided to let her sleep. She can bathe in the morning."

"Yes, and then we'll send her on her way, right?"

"Don't start ordering me around. I'm not a child, nor am I old enough to be delusional. I'm not about to allow someone to come into my home and take advantage of my hospitality. But the girl needs our help. That much is obvious."

"She certainly needs someone's help." But surely that didn't mean they had to take in a wandering soul who could very well have been about to rob them blind.

Mother scowled, then reached for the plates from the cupboard. She set one plate in front of Simon and another for herself. Then she paused and gave him a thoughtful gaze. "From the cut of her clothing, I'd venture to say she comes from quality folk."

"More likely she stole the clothes from someone's home."

"Rubbish."

"Then why is she filthy and peeking into windows?" Simon grabbed an apple fritter from a plate on the table.

"Simon," Mother scolded. "You'll spoil your dinner."

"Not likely. I missed lunch today."

"Why? I packed you two pieces of chicken and two slices of bread."

"I know. I just didn't have time to stop and eat."

"Your father would never have wanted you to work yourself to death to make up for the income lost by his death."

"I know. But expenses are tight."

Mother set the meal on the table with a sigh. "Times are hard for many people."

"Yes," he said pointedly. "Including us."

"The Lord has always provided. We can't allow our lack to dictate whether or not we extend charity—if that's what you're getting at. Say the blessing, please."

Simon complied. They filled their plates in silence; then Mother cleared her throat. "I have something to discuss with you."

A sense of dread filled him. The last time she'd had something to discuss with him, she had invited Mr. and Mrs. Ponch and their daughters—each gunning for a husband—to dinner. That had been a month ago, and Simon still couldn't escape a weekly visit at the bank from each of the young women. It wasn't that there was anything wrong with them. They were pretty enough, good natured, and well-spoken. They just weren't for him. He'd know when the right woman came along. If only his mother could understand that and respect his wishes.

"No more dinners, Mother. Please."

"What? Oh, for pity's sake. I told you I wouldn't invite any more young ladies and their parents over. Although there's not a thing wrong with any of the Ponch girls." She waved to dismiss the thought before he could respond. "Besides, that's not what I want to discuss."

Relief replaced dread, then slid into a healthy caution as Simon eyed his mother. "All right. What do you want to discuss?"

"I have made a decision concerning the house."

Surely Mother wasn't thinking of selling their home. Times were tight but certainly not desperate. "There's no need to think of selling the house."

"Sell the house your father built for me? Never!"

"What, then?"

She gathered a deep breath. "After much prayer, I have decided it is the Lord's will that we receive boarders."

Simon's fork clattered to his plate. "What?" He rose from his chair and paced the kitchen. "Mother. You can't turn our home into a boardinghouse!"

"Of course I can. It's my house."

"It's my home too! I forbid it!"

The uncommon narrowing of Mother's eyes warned Simon that he had gone too far. Her face grew red, and her green eyes sparked with new vitality. "Son," she said slowly, and Simon didn't dare interrupt her to inform her of his rapid change of heart. "I will do whatever the Lord instructs me to do. If He tells me to turn this house into a chicken coop for all the stray chickens in town, that's exactly what I'll do. How dare you forbid me to do anything, young man! Have you forgotten that I diapered your bottom only twenty short years ago?"

Bested, Simon stood, knowing there would be no calming her once she worked herself into a stomping mad fit. He grabbed her hand and bent to kiss her soft, plump cheek. "Forgive me, Mother. I had no right to upset you. But I am less than enthusiastic about the idea."

Patting his hand, Mother gave him an affectionate smile. "You don't have to be enthusiastic about it. But I will need your help once boarders begin to arrive. I've decided to offer our young guest upstairs a small wage and room and board to join our household staff."

"Mother!" Simon released an exasperated breath. "You need to at least ask for references."

"Nonsense. The Lord is all the reference I need. And I believe He sent that child to our doorstep."

"All right. Have it your way. I won't say a word. But that doesn't mean I won't be keeping an eye on her."

And if she made one move that smacked of shadiness,

Simon would haul her to the police station before she could blink an eye.

The sound of a small, nearly panicked voice drifted into the kitchen. "Hello? Is anyone here?"

Simon and Mother exchanged a quick glance, then bolted from the kitchen, through the sitting room, and into the hallway where the "guest" stood trembling at the top of the steps.

"Where am I?"

Simon started to move forward, but Mother stopped him with her arm across his middle. She stepped toward the stairs. "You fainted outside the house, Dear, and my son, Simon, carried you upstairs."

The girl turned wide violet eyes upon Simon and scowled as recognition dawned. "I remember you! You nearly scared the life out of me. What do you mean, sneaking up on people that way?"

Annoyance rose in Simon, heightened by Mother's quick chuckle. Before he could speak, Mother addressed the girl.

"I had planned to let you sleep, but since you're awake, I'll go ahead and draw you a nice hot bath. One of the last things my dear husband did was to install indoor plumbing. I don't know how I ever got along without it."

"Y—you mean, you aren't throwing me out tonight?"

"Well, I should say not." Mother trudged up the steps, huffing by the time she reached the girl. "As a matter of fact, it just so happens we are in the need of a strong young girl such as yourself to help out with household duties. If you are interested, the position is yours."

"Oh!" The girl grabbed onto the railing just in time to keep from plunging headlong down the steps. She sat hard on the landing.

"Are you all right, Dear?"

"Yes, Ma'am. It's just that I never thought He would actually hear my prayer, much less answer so quickly."

Mother gathered the young woman into her arms. "He always hears our prayers. Now, let's get you into the kitchen and get some warm food in your belly."

Simon's heart caught in his throat. Perhaps his mother had been right after all. Had God truly sent this girl to their door? Even so, where had she come from? She was well-spoken, indicative of a high social status. So the questions remained. Why did she look as though she hadn't slept or eaten in days? And why was she running away? Simon didn't like unanswered questions. There were too many of those in his life right now. Somehow he couldn't help but feel that this girl was going to complicate his life, and there was absolutely nothing he could do about it.

two

Torey sank lower into the steaming tub and closed her eyes, still trying to process the fact that she had awakened to such fortunate circumstances. What a marvel that she'd prayed and God had actually answered by sending her to a woman who had taken pity on her.

A niggle of worry wormed through her, however, at the memory of the woman's son. He seemed suspicious. And familiar. She pressed her mind to recall where she'd seen him before, but clarity eluded her. Could he be one of Amos's business associates? Panic raced through her heart. Would he recognize her? Did he already? What if he had already contacted Amos? She sat up, then ducked back under the water as the door opened.

Mrs. Crawford entered the room. "You're not finished already, are you?"

"N—no, Ma'am."

"I thought you might like a little help with washing your lovely hair."

Lovely? Torey had to laugh. After two weeks without benefit of a good brushing—or a poor one, for that matter—her hair was far from lovely.

The woman's eyes twinkled. "I'm seeing it through the eyes of faith."

"The eyes of faith?"

"Lean back, and I'll pour water over your hair."

Torey complied as Mrs. Crawford went on. "The eyes of faith don't look at what something is. . .they see what something—or someone—can become."

"I don't think I have those kind of eyes," Torey murmured. "I wish I did." Reality was often too much to bear. Warm water trickled over her scalp. This reality, on the other hand, felt heavenly. She closed her eyes and could almost imagine that the woman standing over her was her grandmother. Mrs. Crawford was years younger than her grandmother had been, but the manner of speaking was the same. The kindness, the same. The wisdom and understanding. . .the same.

"Faith comes by hearing. And hearing by the Word of God."

"What does that mean?"

"It means if you don't read the Bible and listen to what God speaks to you as you read, you can't have faith. A person who is slack in Bible-reading time will have weak faith."

"That's explains it, then. I haven't opened a Bible since I was eight years old."

"I have extras around here. I'd be happy to loan you one."

"I'd be pleased to borrow it." Not long ago, Torey might have laughed at such a notion as reading the Bible daily. But now she found the idea strangely welcome.

After applying a generous amount of soap to her hair, she scrubbed and scrubbed while Mrs. Crawford busied herself gathering up the filthy, torn clothing Torey had discarded. "I don't think these are worth salvaging," she said, her smile and gentle tone taking the sting from the observation.

"I suppose not, but I have nothing else to wear."

Mrs. Crawford shook her head. "My Georgia married five years ago. She had an entire trousseau made and didn't take a stitch of clothing she wore before she became Mrs. Frank Wesley. I've missed her so much since she moved off that I haven't had the heart to get rid of her clothes."

Torey stopped scrubbing. "Oh, but I can't take. . ."

"Nonsense. What else are you going to wear?" Mrs. Crawford took up the pitcher, and Torey leaned back, once again enjoying the warm water flowing over her scalp. She kept quiet. Indeed, there was nothing to be said. Mrs. Crawford was right. Her clothes were fit only for the ragbag or burning. Sitting up once more in the tub, she took Mrs. Crawford's hand. "Thank you, Ma'am. I appreciate your kindness more than you know."

"Think nothing of it." She scrunched her face into an endearing smile that Torey couldn't help but return. The woman grabbed a large towel and averted her gaze while Torey stood and wrapped herself.

Giving her some privacy to dry off, Mrs. Crawford moved to the other side of the curtain. "Georgia is a bit shorter than you are, but I'm sure we can let the hems out of her dresses enough for them to work until we get you some of your own." Mrs. Crawford handed her a nightdress and a dressing gown over the curtain. "I'm afraid there's nothing we can do about the length of this, unfortunately."

"This will do wonderfully. It's the first clean thing I've worn in two weeks." Torey could have bitten her tongue. She knew the lady would have questions, but she'd hoped to hold her off until she could come up with a believable story—one that was as far from the truth as possible.

She slipped the nightgown over her head and stepped around the privacy curtain. The gown barely covered her calves. But it was warm and wonderfully clean. Torey smiled.

"You're quite a beauty, aren't you?" Mrs. Crawford observed.

Heat crept to Torey's cheeks.

"And modest." Approval shone in her eyes. "If you'll allow me to follow you to your room, I'll help you brush and braid your hair. I imagine if you leave those curls unattended all night, you'll have a mess in the morning."

Torey grinned. "Yes, Ma'am."

They walked down the hall to Torey's room and entered. Once inside, Mrs. Crawford tapped the vanity chair. "All right. You sit down here, and I'll brush your hair like I used to for Georgia."

Doing as she was bidden, Torey sat. Horror filled her as she looked up and captured a glance at herself in the vanity mirror. She gasped at the sight of the almost unrecognizable woman staring back at her. Her eyes, once vibrant, drooped with fatigue and were circled with dark smudges. "Oh, my." Her cheeks looked positively sunken from the weight she'd lost, and her once-rosy complexion looked bleached. Unable to endure yet another shock to her overtaxed nerves, she burst into tears.

Mrs. Crawford knelt beside her and pulled her into warm, comforting arms. "I have a feeling you've been through a very difficult time. Would you like to talk about it?"

"No," she wailed. "I can't."

"All right. I won't push you. But I need to know. . .have you done something illegal?"

Torey stopped crying and pulled away. "I–I don't think so." Fresh tears assaulted her. "Amos said I'm as guilty as he is. But I'm just not sure."

"And what did Amos do, Honey?"

Her mellow tone calmed Torey. She was so tired of running. So tired. And if trouble was going to visit this wonderful woman because of her, she'd rather just come clean now and take what she had coming. Gathering a deep breath for courage, Torey shuddered, reliving the scene as she remembered it. "I–I saw my stepfather m–murder a man."

"Oh, you poor thing!" Mrs. Crawford patted her shoulder as a fresh onslaught of tears spilled over. When Torey calmed, the older woman pulled away and handed her a hanky. "Now, let's go over this. Were you privy to his intentions prior to his actions?"

Torey shook her head. "B–but I saw it happen and I didn't, that is I couldn't. . .I wanted to scream and warn that poor man, but it all happened so fast. . . ."

"Of course, there was nothing you could do. Your stepfather threatened you, I presume?"

"Y—yes."

"That's the reason for your appearance here, then? You are running from him?"

Torey nodded.

"Why didn't you go to the police?"

"I—Amos said that I'm an ac—accessory and will get the same punishment as him."

"Hogwash."

Glancing into the woman's eyes, Torey saw anger flashing in their depths. "I won't go to jail?"

Mrs. Crawford placed her hands on Torey's shoulders and resumed brushing. "Let's start at the beginning, and you tell me who you are and what happened. Then I'll be in a better position to advise."

Hesitating only a brief amount of time, Torey drew in a breath and launched into the wretched story, leaving out no detail of that horrible night, beginning with Amos escorting her to the opera with no warning and ending when she broke away and ran from the theatre and Amos's clutches.

"You saw this happen at the theatre?" Mrs. Crawford's voice was hoarse.

"Yes, Ma'am. I am so sorry. I've upset you with the gruesomeness of this crime."

Face drained of all color, Mrs. Crawford set the brush on the vanity, her hands trembling. Her lips moved, and Torey wondered if she was praying or if she'd suddenly gone daft.

Self-deprecation slammed into Torey's heart, silently berating her for upsetting the poor woman. She stood. "I'll leave tonight," she said. Her lips trembled as she reached for the filthy clothing, which was thrown in a pile next to the door.

Mrs. Crawford roused and glanced at her sharply. "Now listen here. You will do nothing of the kind."

"I don't want to cause you any trouble. You've been kinder than anyone has been to me in a very long time." Since her mother had died.

"Put your mind to rest about that, my girl." She hedged a moment, and Torey held her breath until the woman resumed her thoughts. "Let's keep this information between just the two of us for now."

"You mean you don't think I should go to the police?"

"As much as I'm inclined to send you right over to the station, I believe it's best if we keep this quiet." Her eyes misted. "You're safe here. We'll wait on God's timing for you to reveal what you've told me tonight. Come, you are exhausted. Why don't you crawl into bed?"

Unbidden, a yawn stretched Torey's mouth. She nodded. "You're right."

Mrs. Crawford turned down the covers, and Torey slid between the cotton sheets. Her eyes closed as though of their own volition. Then they popped open again at a sudden thought. She sat up.

Mrs. Crawford stooped and gathered Torey's old clothes.

"Mrs. Crawford?"

"Yes?"

"You said you need domestic help?"

"Yes, and we'd like you to have the job."

By *we*, Torey knew Mrs. Crawford wasn't referring to her son. His eyes had narrowed in suspicion every time he looked at her while she ate her meal. He'd peppered her with questions until his mother had put a stop to it. Torey didn't blame him. He wasn't necessarily wrong to be suspicious.

"You've been so good to me, I feel I need to be honest."

"What is it?" The woman shifted her weight from one foot to the next but stayed in position by the door.

Heat crept to Torey's face. "The fact is that I don't know how to do anything."

"Of course you do." Mrs. Crawford waved her concern aside. "Everyone knows how to do something."

Torey frowned, worry seeping through her. Mrs. Crawford obviously couldn't fathom that someone would be unable to do the smallest of household chores, but the fact of the matter was that Torey had had servants her entire life. She had never intended to lift her hand to wash a dish or make a bed or scrub a floor. Of course, Mrs. Crawford was right, though. She wasn't completely inept. "Well, I am quite handy with a needle. And before she passed on, my mama always complimented my endeavors with a paintbrush. But as for domestic work. . ."

"You'll learn," Mrs. Crawford said firmly; then she stopped and peered closer at Torey. "Unless for some reason you don't *want* the job."

"Oh, no! I do want it. As long as you understand that I will have to be taught my duties before I can perform them."

A smile curved the older woman's lips. "I understand."

"And if I can't do the job or perform poorly, I will leave without delay."

Mrs. Crawford opened the door. "You'll do fine. As a matter of fact, I have a feeling you'll take to the work quite naturally and will master it in no time."

"How can you be so sure?"

"Remember those eyes of faith?"

"Yes. But I confess that I don't understand."

"Faith is the substance of things hoped for. The evidence of things that are yet to be seen. So when I look at you, I see the fine housemaid you're going to become. Not the sleepy girl who can't boil an egg."

"Oh, I can do that!"

A chuckle shook the woman's large frame. "Well, see? You're already one step ahead. Now, I'm going to turn down the lamp and let you get some rest."

Torey smiled and stretched back onto the mattress. "Good night."

The door closed behind her. Torey turned to the window and watched the stars outside. Her heavy eyelids closed, but she opened them once more, fighting to stay awake for just a minute longer so she could enjoy the soft bed and warm covers—the first moment of peace she'd known since that terrible night. She thought of the alleyways and parks where she'd been sleeping for a few minutes at a time over the past two weeks. She could almost feel the gnawing hunger she'd experienced every minute of that time, despite the food she'd wolfed down only an hour before. She'd been too hungry to wait until after her bath.

Her heart swelled with contentment. Too sleepy to voice the words in her heart, she sent a silent prayer into the night. *Thank You for answering me so quickly.*

ะ

At the sound of creaking steps outside the library door, Simon tossed aside the book he'd been attempting to read.

"Mother?" he called. He stood and met her in the hallway. "May we discuss this, please?"

"Discuss what?"

"I want to discuss the girl, of course." Simon frowned at the rags in his mother's arms. "I'll follow you into the kitchen so you can discard those things."

"All right." A weary sigh lifted her bosom. "What about Torey Mitchell would you like to discuss?"

"Torey?"

"Short for Victoria."

"What else have you learned about her?"

"Enough to strengthen my position. God sent her here."

Releasing a heavy sigh, Simon decided retreat was the best form of defense at the moment. "All right. Have it your way. Did you tell her what her duties will be?"

Mother scowled. "She's worn through and through. I plan to give her as many days as she needs to rest from her ordeal. And when she is ready, I'll begin instructing her in doing household tasks."

"Instructing?" Simon planted his feet. "Are you telling me our new maid doesn't know how to take care of a home?"

"She'll learn. We'll need to be patient for a few days." Her eyes took on a gentle expression. "Wasn't the Lord good to bring Torey soon enough to learn her job before we open the house to boarders?"

"Sure. Sure." He raked his fingers through his hair, which he was certain was growing gray by the second. "All right, Mother. I can see you've made up your mind."

"Quite."

"Give me those things, and I'll take them out and burn them." He motioned toward the filthy garments his mother still held.

"You go and build the fire. I'll throw them in. Torey would be humiliated by the thought of a man handling some of these things."

Heat crept up his neck. "Oh."

"Simon. You really must trust me. The Lord sent her to us. Get to know her. You'll see. . ."

Narrowing his eyes in suspicion, he studied her. "Mother. . ."

"Yes?"

Not one whit fooled by her look of utter innocence, Simon regarded her firmly. "Do *not* try to pair me off with this new maid."

Mother gave a self-righteous sniff and jerked her chin. "I'm sure I don't have a notion what you're talking about."

"I'm sure you *do* have a notion. It was bad enough when you were throwing me at eligible young ladies—daughters of business associates of Father's."

"Some of whom were quite nice."

"Nevertheless, choosing my wife is my own affair, and I'll thank you to leave me to it." Honoring and respecting one's mother was one thing. But at a certain age a man had to put his foot down.

Puffing out her cheeks, Mother crossed her arms. Her eyes flashed her outrage. "Well, I've never tried to choose for you. But there's nothing wrong with a mother providing the supply *from* which to choose."

"And do you honestly believe I will fall in love with a member of the staff?"

"It's been known to happen."

"Not to me." Though the thought of the girl's lovely eyes and the memory of her relief when she'd discovered she was to stay shot through his heart, bringing out his protective nature in a way he'd never felt for a young lady. But a man didn't build a relationship upon compassion.

"I thought we agreed you weren't going to be snobbish."

Mother's words brought him back from thoughts of Torey. "All right, Mother. I won't be snobbish." He smiled. "But I won't be falling in love with our new maid either. I like short girls."

"Rubbish. You need a woman who can look you in the eye and give you what for."

Opening the door, he gave her a half grin. "Sure I do." About as much as he needed an itchy rash. "I'm going to go build that fire."

He walked outside. What had brought the girl to such desperate circumstances? Mother knew something. And she wasn't talking.

Whatever it was, he only hoped it didn't spell trouble for them. They'd had enough heartache to last a lifetime.

❧

Amos pulled at the handlebars of his moustache and eyed the man in front of him. At seventy-plus years, John Shepherd still cut an imposing figure, even if he was dwarfed between the two thugs who accompanied him wherever he went.

"I've been patient," John said evenly. "Extremely patient."

"I know," Amos said, glad he was standing a desk away from the apes on either side of John.

John raised his brow to silence him. Amos clamped his lips shut.

"Perhaps you mistakenly believed the sizeable amount of money I loaned you was a gift."

Amos opened his mouth but quickly shut it again at the glare he received as John went on. "But then, how can that be when you agreed to pay it back, with interest—and by last week?"

"I know, and I fully intended—"

"We seem to have a problem. I loaned you that sum in good faith. Now I find I can't trust you to keep your end of a business venture."

Fear shot through Amos. He eyed the "apes," imagining himself beaten to a pulp first by one, then the other.

"If you can just give me a few more days, I—"

"You'll what?" John gave a short laugh, devoid of humor. "I happen to know you owe practically all of my associates and some of my competitors."

Nearly strangled with fear, Amos seriously considered falling to his knees and begging for mercy. If he thought it might help, nothing could have kept him from it. He knew, however, that John had no mercy. And when the wicked old miser was finished toying with him, he'd sic the apes on him, and Amos would be nothing but a memory.

He gathered a deep shaky breath and decided to die with as much dignity as he could muster. "All right, Mr. Shepherd. You're right. I can't outrun you. I can't hide from the eyes you have all over this city and beyond. You might as well go ahead and kill me, because you know I can't pay you back."

John again raised his brow, this time in what appeared to be surprise. "Come now, you misunderstand. I have a proposition for you."

Relief flooded Amos, and to his horror, tears pricked his eyes. "Anything. I'll do whatever you want me to do."

A nearly toothless grin split the old face. "Then it appears your troubles are over."

three

Torey popped her burning finger into her mouth and attempted to keep from crying out. Ironing Simon's shirts was the bane of her existence as a maid. Already she'd burned three of her fingers, scorched two of his shirts; and the two shirts she had managed to keep from scorching had more wrinkles ironed *in* than she'd actually ironed out in the first place.

Why didn't he just wear his jacket buttoned? Then no one would notice whether his shirts had wrinkles or not—and it would greatly lessen Torey's load.

Mrs. Crawford had been patient thus far, but Torey worried the woman would soon grow tired of her ineptness and throw her into the street. At the disturbing thought, she attacked the wrinkles with new determination. Ironing would not beat her into submission. If other women could accomplish the feat, so could she. It was just a matter of putting her mind to it and concentrating. First one section, then the next.

"Good morning, Miss Mitchell."

Torey jumped as Simon's unusually cheerful voice preceded him into the room. With a cry from the pain searing the heel of her hand, she flung the iron onto the board. "Oh!" Trying not to burst into tears, she cradled her arm to her waist.

"Are you all right?"

Torey returned his gaze, hot words of outrage over his sudden, unsettling appearance on her lips. The concern in his eyes stopped the spill, and she nodded. "I will be."

"I'm so sorry I caused you to burn yourself." He held out his hand. "Let me take a look."

Reluctantly, she showed him her palm.

A frowned creased his brow. "This looks terrible."

Torey followed his gaze to her hand. On every finger, an angry blister mocked her, promising to become an ugly scar or callous. She sighed. Her hands would never again be smooth, white, and unblemished.

"You only caused this one." She pointed to a newly forming blister. "My hand slipped from the iron handle when you startled me."

"I'm sorry. I just arrived home from work and was looking for my mother. I smelled dinner cooking and thought. . ."

"Oh. She's not in here." Heat burned Torey's cheeks as she stated the obvious for want of anything else to respond.

"I can see that." He stood so close, Torey could have touched him without reaching. His warm fingers still wrapped around her wrist, and his attention was focused on her burns. Torey caught her breath as he looked away from her hand and captured her gaze. "You can't work with those blisters."

"They're nothing, really." As a matter of fact, she barely felt the pain at all for the moment.

Abruptly, he turned his head. "Do you smell that?"

An acrid stench filled the air. Torey gasped. She snatched her hand away from Simon and made a grab for the iron. With a groan, she pulled it off yet another ruined shirt. This one was beyond scorched. She gave a defeated shrug and lifted the shirt from the board. "You can take the cost to replace this shirt—a–and two more—out of my salary."

His chuckle surprised her. She met his gaze. Gray eyes twinkled in amusement.

Irritation bit at her. "You think it's funny that I'm ruining all your clothes?"

He raised his eyebrows. "No. Well, yes. I'm sorry. I guess I do find it a little humorous."

Torey gave a sniff. "Well, I don't. Th–this ironing is so

difficult. I never realized how hard Beatrice worked to ensure my clothes were properly cared for and presentable. She never burned even one of my gowns, and look. . .I can't even iron a simple shirt."

"Beatrice?" His expression bespoke more than mere curiosity. Torey cringed inwardly. She'd rather see the twinkle of humor than the raw suspicion now shooting from his eyes. "Who was Beatrice?"

"Someone I used to know. That's all."

"You've been here for a week, Miss Mitchell. Surely you know by now that you can tell us if you're in trouble."

"Leave her alone, Simon."

Torey nearly fainted in relief as Simon's mother came into the kitchen.

"H—hello, Mrs. Crawford."

"Hello, my dear." She smiled broadly. "I came to see how you are faring with the ironing."

"N—not very well, I'm afraid."

"I can see that." Mrs. Crawford drew her bottom lip between her teeth. "Ironing might not be your strong suit."

"I'm sorry, Ma'am. Please take the cost of the shirts from my salary."

"Don't be silly. Everyone scorches clothes when they first start ironing. We'll move on to learning another chore." Once more, she glanced at the shirts. "Dusting, maybe," she muttered.

"We were just about to get something to dress her burns, Mother. She'd probably better not try to work the rest of the day."

"Burns?" Mrs. Crawford glanced sharply at Torey's hands. "What burns?"

"They're nothing, really," Torey said, though the throbbing fingers and stinging palm testified to her fib.

"Let me see."

She complied.

"Oh, my." Shaking her head, Mrs. Crawford clucked her tongue. "I blame myself entirely. I should never have left you alone with an unfamiliar chore. Of course we must dress those burns, and you'll need to rest your hands for several days while you heal."

"Oh, no, Ma'am. I can still work."

"No, Honey. You can't. Putting your hands in water or soap would burn like fire, and you can't work one-handed." She turned to Simon. "Take one of those shirts and cut it into strips, please. No sense letting that cloth go to waste when we can make perfectly good bandages out of it."

From the corner of her eye, Torey saw Simon lift a shirt from the ironing board. She could feel his gaze upon her, but she didn't look at him. If she did, would she find condemnation? More suspicion? Interest? The last thought sent butterfly wings flapping through her stomach.

"Should I tear up the rest of these, Mother?" he asked, with a hint of something that was probably sarcasm—or possibly humor. Either way, the question itself testified to her dismal lack of ability.

Tears pricked her eyes. "I'm so sorry. I'll leave immediately." She looked down at her borrowed dress. "I don't know how I'll get this back to you or what condition it will be in."

"What are you talking about? I don't want you to quit. God hasn't gifted all of us in the same things, and apparently ironing isn't one of your gifts." Mrs. Crawford walked across the room and took a jar of salve from a cabinet above the stove. "You can't help that."

Torey followed her. "It just isn't right for you to have a maid who can't do the things maids do. It would be better for you if I simply go away and let you hire someone who can do the work."

"Come on over to the table and have a seat so I can have a look at that hand."

Doing as she was bidden, Torey rested her arm on the table with her palm up.

"I want to make one thing very clear." Mrs. Crawford gently took Torey's wrist but eyed her sternly.

"Yes, Ma'am?"

"I know in my heart the Lord sent you to me. I needed help, and so did you. We'll have no more talk of you leaving, for now. When God is ready for you to move on, He'll let us both know, but it certainly won't be for something as trivial as a few scorched shirts."

Torey couldn't resist stealing a peek at Simon. He observed her, his eyes narrowed, studying her. A strange sense of familiarity once more flitted through Torey. She had definitely seen him before. . .but where?

&

"Turn it loose, you. . .you beast!"

Simon roused from his sleep with a start.

"You don't scare me! I said let go immediately before I slap your nose!"

Slap your nose?

Fully awake, Simon's curiosity got the better of him. He slid out of bed and grabbed his dressing gown, putting it on as he walked to the window.

The ruckus on the ground below lifted a chuckle from his throat. The neighborhood menace had escaped his home once again. Abe, an enormous St. Bernard named for the late president, had escaped from the Nelsons' home three doors down.

Simon had to admire Torey's spirit. Even from his vantage point he could see her trembling. She must be too terrified of the dog's massive size to notice Abe's tail flopping around behind him as he played wrestle-the-wet-sheet-from-the-pretty-maid.

"You bad, bad dog." Her voice broke. "You're ruining everything! I finally have the hang of something, and you have to go and rip his sheets? How will I ever explain this to Mr. High and Mighty? Bad enough I ruined his shirts and broke his favorite coffee mug."

"Mr. High and Mighty?" Was that what she thought of him? Guilt shot through Simon. He had been a little suspicious, and rightfully so under the circumstances, but he didn't realize he'd been acting "high and mighty."

The title didn't sit well with him, and the more he considered it, the less he liked it. Was he snobbish as Mother always admonished him not to be? The idea bothered him more than he'd thought possible. It was bad enough that anyone would consider him less than friendly, but it disturbed him particularly that the pretty young woman, who at this moment was straining against a mammoth dog, felt so.

Making a firm decision, he ducked out of the window and to the wardrobe across the room. Perhaps the time had come to modify his image. After all, the girl had been in their employ for two weeks, and nothing but a few household mishaps had occurred. There was every chance that she had simply run away from a bad situation and God had sent her to them as Mother insisted was the case.

Knowing Abe would never hurt Torey, Simon refrained from calling down and alerting them to his eavesdropping. Instead, he dressed and hurried down the stairs and out the back door. As he'd suspected would be the case, Abe and Torey still struggled over the now-shredded sheet.

"Good morning," he said with all the cheerful goodwill he could muster.

Abe turned the sheet loose at the sound of Simon's voice, and Torey flew backward. Her scream raked the air as Simon watched in horror, unable to move fast enough to spare her a hard landing on the dewy ground.

Fending off Abe's paws, Simon hurried to Torey and reached down. "Let me help you up."

Ignoring his hand, she stared at the mangled sheet, not only shredded but smudged with dirt as well.

"Well, looks like we won't be running out of bandages any time soon," Simon quipped, then bit back laughter as she glared up at him.

"What's that supposed to mean?"

"Nothing. I just. . .I'd hoped to make you smile."

She sniffed. "It's not working."

"I can see that. Please accept my apology." He gave a pointed glance to his still-stretched-out arm. "And my help up from there."

Her cheeks pinkened. "Oh. Of course. Thank you." She slipped her hand in his and allowed herself to be lifted off the ground. Abe immediately grabbed the sheet once more.

"No! You dumb animal!" Torey's voice trembled.

"Come here, Abe," Simon said with firmness in his voice. "I think you've caused enough trouble for one day." The dog obeyed and let the sheet go once more. This time, Torey managed to stay on her feet.

"You know this monster?"

"He belongs a couple of doors down."

"Well, they should keep him tied up," she said, smoothing down her skirt.

He chuckled. "They usually do. He breaks free every once in awhile. If you'll hand me the sheet, I'll make a lead for him and take him back where he belongs."

Compassion rose inside of Simon at the shame creeping over her features. He hunkered down and tied a strip of the torn sheet around Abe's neck. "You know, this isn't your fault. You have nothing to apologize for."

Surprise lifted her silky brows. "Thank you, Mr. Crawford."

His heart soared. "You're most welcome, Miss Mitchell."

She turned back to her task and lifted another sheet from her basket. She kept a close eye on the dog—who, even

Simon had to admit, looked as though he'd like nothing better than to play the game again.

Suddenly feeling all arms and legs, as though he were a twelve-year-old boy, Simon cleared his throat. "Well, good day, Miss Mitchell," he said, tugging on the makeshift leash.

"Good day, Mr. Crawford. Thank you for coming to my rescue."

Again, his heart soared. He smiled and nodded, then led the dog toward his own home. Halfway down the block, he met Frank, the Nelsons' gardener.

"Lose something?" Simon asked.

A scowl creased the already-lined face. "That animal is a menace," the old man said, shaking his head. "Always bothering the neighbors."

"Other than our flustered maid and a torn sheet, there was no harm done," Simon said, handing over the makeshift leash.

"Don't suppose there's any sense in returning this to you."

Simon chuckled. "I don't suppose so."

"Sorry for the inconvenience. I'll try to see that he doesn't get out again." The grizzled man turned to leave, then stopped and turned back.

"I was wondering. . ."

"Yes?"

"This might not be any of my business, but did you get some visitors?"

"No. Mother is getting the house ready to take in boarders, but no one has moved in yet."

The man nodded but didn't reply. His action raised Simon's curiosity. "Why do you ask?"

He shrugged. "I noticed a man in your yard last night around dusk. Never saw him before. I just thought you might have a visitor."

The news unsettled Simon more than just a little. He frowned. "What did the man look like?"

"Not sure. Like I said, it was getting dark, and my eyes have grown a bit dim with age. He was a tall man; that much I could see. Not fat but not small."

"And what was he doing in our yard? Was he trying to get into the house?"

"Not that I noticed. He was just standing there, looking at the house with his hands in his trouser pockets."

"Thank you for telling me, Frank. And if you see him again, could you let me know?"

The man's eyes narrowed. "You think he might have been up to no good?"

"I think it best not to take any chances."

"I'll keep a lookout for him."

"Thank you."

Simon walked away, worry spreading through him. What if Father's murderer hadn't been a simple thief as the police believed? What if he intended Mother harm as well?

The thought was intolerable, and Simon stepped up his pace, glad he had the weekend off from the bank. The smell of breakfast cooking led him to the kitchen, where he found his mother standing over the stove, frying bacon.

"Where's Katherine?"

The aging housekeeper had been taking care of the Crawfords for as long as Simon could remember.

"Feeling poorly today. I sent her back upstairs." She shot him a look. "Torey is hanging clothes on the line, if you're wondering why she isn't fixing breakfast instead of me."

"I know. I saw her."

"You did?"

Impatiently, Simon relayed the tale, his amusement with the entire situation shadowed by his concern over Frank's news.

"Mother, I want to hire a man to protect the house while I'm away at work."

Turning to set a platter down on the table, his mother gave

him a look that plainly said she thought he'd lost his mind.

"Frank noticed a strange man standing in the yard, staring at the house the other night."

"Maybe it was someone who heard we had rooms to let and decided he didn't like the looks of the place."

"I doubt it."

"We can't afford to hire a silly bodyguard."

"Mother, just suppose Father's murder wasn't a simple robbery. What if there was an agenda, and the killer is still looking for something? Wouldn't the logical thing be to look at the house?"

Mother stopped and seemed to consider his words. "All right."

"You mean it?" Simon had planned to implement his plan anyway, but he felt better knowing his mother agreed.

She nodded. "I agree that we need to pray for God to send the person He wants for the job."

With an exasperated sigh, Simon took his seat at the table. "Mother, there are professionals who are in the business of protecting those who pay their salaries. I was thinking of looking into one of those. Maybe a retired police officer or boxer or something."

"And if that's what the Lord has in mind, then I'm sure He'll send one."

"Sometimes you can't just wait. Sometimes God gives you the insight and expects you to do your part."

Mother finished setting the food on the table and took her place across from Simon. "Son, I know we can't always wait. But I believe God wants to send the right person to protect our home. Can't we wait just a few days?"

"The danger is now."

"Then God will work it out sooner."

"I'll be here to protect you over the weekend, but if God hasn't sent someone by Monday, I'm finding someone."

"Fair enough."

They bowed their heads and said the blessing. But Simon's mind went back to the image of a stranger watching his home. He wondered if Torey were involved in some sort of ill intentions against him and his mother. They already knew the girl wasn't a maid. Yet she'd accepted the position without so much as thinking it over. She'd arrived on their doorstep unkempt and in obvious need a mere two weeks after Father's death. A respectable amount of time. What if she and her accomplice had planned it? Played on Mother's sympathies? He didn't want to believe it, but he couldn't help but return to his former suspicions. Better to be "Mr. High and Mighty" and keep his distance than to be played the fool and possibly cause his mother more heartache. Or worse.

The door opened, and Torey walked in carrying her laundry basket. Simon's heart lurched. He swallowed hard, admitting to himself that his resolution might be harder to keep than he suspected, especially when she turned her gorgeous violet eyes upon him. A shy smile lifted the corners of her lips.

"Good morning, Miss Mitchell," he said as though he hadn't just rescued her from Abe a few minutes earlier.

"Katherine is feeling poorly. Please take her a tray, and then assume her duties for the day."

"Simon!" Mother scowled.

"I'm sorry, Mother, but there are chores that need to be done, and you and I are going to Aunt Elizabeth's, remember?"

"Oh, that's right. I'd forgotten. I'd better finish up quickly and pack my dinner clothes." She glanced at Torey, whose face looked unsettlingly stricken. "Torey dear, Simon and I will not be here for dinner this evening. There is stew left over in the icebox. Please warm it up for yours and Katherine's supper."

"Yes, Ma'am. Should I ask Katherine which chores she would like me to attend to? Or do you have a list for me?"

"Just finish the laundry. That's plenty of work for one day."

Torey lifted her gaze to Simon, then quickly looked away.

Simon tried not to watch her as she prepared the house-keeper's tray, but he found himself drawn by her graceful movements. She stood like a princess. His gaze went to the curve of her neck where wisps of blond hair brushed against her skin. His mouth went dry, and he fought the urge to go and apologize. A painful kick in the shin brought him to his senses.

He jerked his gaze to his mother. A deep scowl lined her brow. They remained silent until Torey excused herself and carried the breakfast tray from the kitchen.

"You can't have it both ways, Simon."

"What do you mean?"

"Torey's a lovely girl. Inside and out. But you can't admire her beauty as a woman and treat her like a maid."

"She *is* a maid," he reminded her.

"Yes, but you treat her as though you suspect her of some-thing. You need to settle your heart and mind about her before you let her know you also admire her. Otherwise there is potential for her to be hurt."

Simon placed his napkin on the table and stood. "All right, Mother. From now on, I will act as though I don't even know our lovely Miss Mitchell is in the room."

"I think that's for the best."

"If you'll excuse me, I will go and dress for our trip across town."

Torey was descending the steps just as he was going up. She kept her gaze away from him, and Simon realized she'd gotten the message. A curious disappointment filled him. What would be the end result of her presence in his home?

four

Torey finished putting away the last of the dishes, satisfied that at least she could do that much and not cause a catastrophe. After three days without breaking a dish, she was beginning to feel confident in this particular chore.

The house felt empty without Mrs. Crawford and Simon. Katherine's illness had kept the elderly housekeeper abed all day, and now Torey found herself at loose ends. After wiping down all the counters, sweeping the kitchen floor, and ensuring herself that everything sparkled, she wandered into the library. Mrs. Crawford had said she might read whatever books she'd like, but thus far she'd been too busy concentrating on learning her tasks to take advantage of the offer. And she had been too exhausted at the end of each day to do anything but fall into bed.

She perused the shelves, delighted with the vast selection of books by her favorite authors: Jane Austen, Emily Brontë, Charles Dickens, and a variety of poets. She even noticed with guilty glee a few selections by the irreverent Mark Twain. A surge of joy shot through her as she scanned the shelves, and she couldn't decide which to choose. She enjoyed love stories. Particularly the kind where a girl of unfortunate circumstances fell in love with the lord of the manor, and of course those feelings were always reciprocated. Simon's face intruded upon her mind, and she imagined him to be a hero of one of those books and herself to be the heroine. Heat burned her cheeks at the thought, but she couldn't resist allowing herself the small dream.

During the past two weeks, she'd tried not to venture too many glances his way, had tried to still her racing heart anytime he came near. Over and over she relived the moment he'd held her wrist and examined her burns. And her stomach flip-flopped every time she thought of him coming to her rescue from the monster dog that morning. The way he'd looked at her had nearly melted her insides, and she had been sure he would be asking to court her. She frowned. The puzzlement had come when she walked inside to find Simon and Mrs. Crawford eating breakfast. He'd acted as though she were nothing more than a maid. As though he hadn't just rescued her and smiled at her in such a way as to make her believe he thought her to be remarkable. But then, how was he to know that she'd grown up in a house twice as grand as this one? How was he to know that two weeks ago, a simple bank clerk would never have been allowed to court her. He couldn't know. Ever. And if the truth be told, she much preferred living as a maid in this wonderful household than living in privilege in a murderer's home.

She only wished she could have the chance to apologize to Beatrice for all the times she'd been insensitive. Not that she'd ever been cruel or rude to her maid, but she'd never considered the work the young woman did. Beatrice had lived in the house and had spent every waking hour, except for her one day off each week, seeing to Torey's needs.

What was Beatrice doing now that Torey was gone? Amos had no need of a woman's maid. Had he thrown her out on the street? It was doubtful she would have any desire to stay without Torey in the house. She never seemed comfortable when Amos was near. Torey had long suspected Amos of showing the handsome maid unwelcome attention.

A humiliating thought brought a gasp to her lips. Was Simon the type of man to dally with his servants as well?

Surely he wasn't the same sort as Amos in that respect. Oh! Had she esteemed him higher than he deserved? Better that he act superior and treat her as though she were invisible than to trifle with her heart when they were alone and pretend she didn't exist when they were in anyone else's company.

Armed with this new suspicion, she tried to push him from her mind and concentrate on finding an appropriate book to read—one without romance. When her gaze came to rest on the Bible, her choice was made, and Simon's intentions forgotten. She couldn't have chosen anything else. What had Mrs. Crawford said to her that first night? *"A person who is slack in Bible-reading time will have weak faith."*

Torey admired Mrs. Crawford more than she'd ever admired anyone in her life, except her own grandmother. If reading the Bible would give her the kind of outlook on life her benefactress had, she would read it from cover to cover as many times as possible before she died. She smiled and settled into a wing chair before the fireplace. She was grateful the weather remained warm despite the autumn season. She wouldn't have known how to build and maintain a fire and felt quite sure she would have burned down the house had she attempted such a feat.

A white slip of paper peeked out from the top of the closed Bible. Torey opened to that point, gathered a long breath, and began to read the Gospel of Luke. The story was familiar, yet she somehow felt she'd never heard it before. She'd known from childhood of the miraculous birth of Jesus, how God protected Him as a baby so He wouldn't die before the appointed time. She knew that He died on the cross, but she'd never thought about it as much more than a story from history.

As a girl, she had knelt beside her grandmother and repeated a prayer to ask Jesus into her heart, but as years without Christian influence had gone by, she'd all but forgotten that short year of daily prayer and Bible stories under her grandmother's watchful tending to her spiritual condition.

Now, as she read the account of the death of Jesus, tears streamed down her face. Understanding, like a sudden light, pushed back her cloudy images of what Jesus must have endured. She saw clearly that He had lived and died for her sins. And as she internalized His sacrifice, she dropped to her knees in front of the chair, as she'd seen Mrs. Crawford doing that first night. She was alone, yet she felt as though perhaps God was sitting beside her, urging her on.

She prayed from her heart and hoped that He would hear her. "Jesus, thank You for dying for me. I never seriously thought about how terrible it must have been for You to be beaten and nailed to a cross." She could barely speak through the sobs. "My life isn't much, but such as it is, I give it to You. I want to belong to You. I want to be kind like Mrs. Crawford has been to me. And I want to see with the eyes of faith, like she told me about. Oh, God, I want to be the sort of woman my grandmother wanted me to be."

She stayed on her knees, weeping as she repented of her sins and praised God for hearing her prayer and allowing her to stay at the Crawfords' home.

Lifting her apron, she wiped her eyes, a smile touching her lips. She rested her cheek on her hands and closed her eyes again, reveling in the newness she felt.

For the first time since her mother's death three years earlier, Torey felt as though she wasn't alone.

&

"Mother, at least consider the option."

Mrs. Crawford shook her head firmly and narrowed her gaze at Simon as light from the streetlamps streamed through the carriage window.

"I do not need to hire a detective to investigate Torey."

"Sometimes you are altogether too trusting." Helpless frustration kept a steady clutch on Simon's heart. "After Frank told me that a man has been skulking about our yard, I should think you would be more cautious."

Mother gave a wave and a sniff. "It is highly unlikely one has to do with the other. Where is your faith?"

"Faith is one thing," he shot back. "Carelessness is another."

Her expression softened. "I know you are only trying to protect me, Simon dear. But you must believe me when I tell you, the Lord is looking out for us. Torey told me her story the first night she arrived."

"She did?" Simon perked up, waiting for his mother to relay the information.

"Yes."

After a long silence, it was apparent to Simon that his mother had no intention of being forthcoming. Releasing a long breath, he averted his gaze and stared unseeingly out the window. They were almost home. Leaving Torey had been a test of sorts as far as he was concerned. Would they find the girl and half of their possessions missing when they arrived?

"Mother, how do you know she was telling the truth? Has it occurred to you that she might have concocted a story to lure you into feeling sympathy for her?"

"No. To tell you the truth, it never crossed my mind. I know when someone is lying to me, and Torey was being honest." She smiled. "You get to know her, and you'll see what I mean."

A smile twisted his lips. "I thought you told me to leave her alone."

"I meant don't trifle with her. She's been through enough, and if I'm not mistaken, she's already taken with you. You could easily break her heart."

His pulse quickened. "Do you think so?"

"Ahh, so you're taken with her as well."

Heat crept up his neck. "She intrigues me. Probably because I don't know anything about her."

"The air of mystery."

"Exactly."

"Hmm, maybe." She shrugged. "It probably doesn't have anything to do with beautiful blue eyes—"

"Closer to violet." Simon could have bitten his tongue.

"Oh, you've noticed?" his mother asked, a smug smile on her lips.

"Apparently." And perhaps it did have something to do with her eyes and her golden hair that just that morning had shimmered in the newly risen sun. The tender curve of her neck, the slight tilt of her head when she was concentrating hard to perform a task correctly—combined, they created a fetching picture. One that was difficult to shake.

His mother cleared her throat, drawing him from the lovely image in his mind. He scowled. "All right. Perhaps there is a lot to admire about the girl. But that doesn't diminish the fact that we know nothing about her."

"I do."

"Well, I don't. And since you don't appear compelled to share your knowledge with me, you leave me no choice but to hire an investigator on my own."

Anger flashed in his mother's eyes. "Now, Simon. You're a grown man, and I can't force your obedience any longer. But I am asking you to trust my judgment and leave it alone for now. Torey has been through enough."

It was difficult to look at her and refuse her to her face. Whatever ordeal Torey had endured couldn't be any worse than what his mother had suffered in the past month. But the anger had receded from her eyes, and in its place an entreaty shone silently: *Trust me.*

He reached forward and took her hand. "All right, Mother. You win. I won't look into Torey's past. But I insist upon hiring the guard for the house."

"Only if God doesn't send someone before Monday, remember? You promised."

"I remember." He began making plans in his mind for hiring the guard. After all, who was going to show up for an unadvertised position in the next thirty-six hours?

The hackney turned onto their street. Again Simon's stomach turned, wondering what they'd find when they arrived home.

Moments later, he paid the hacker and carried their bags up the steps. He opened the door for his mother. Relief that everything seemed in place combined with a curious disappointment that Torey wasn't on hand to greet them. In all fairness, he had to admit that she'd probably enjoyed her day to herself and had most likely gone to bed early.

"Good night, Mother," he said after ensuring the door was secure.

"Good night, Son," she replied, offering her cheek for his kiss. "I see the library light is still burning."

"I'll douse it. You go on up to bed."

"Thank you." She headed for the steps, and Simon walked into the library. He was just about to turn down the gas lamps on the wall when he heard a sound coming from somewhere near the cold fireplace. With a frown, he walked cautiously to his favorite wing chair. He caught his breath at the sight that met his eyes.

"Oh, Simon, I forgot—"

He turned quickly toward the door and placed his finger on his lips to silence his mother. At her frown, he pointed down at the sleeping maid. She sat on the floor, as though she'd been in prayer, her cheek rested on her folded arms. A Bible lay in the seat, open to the Gospel of Luke.

Simon swallowed hard as he studied Torey's sleeping face. Her long lashes brushed her tearstained cheeks. Even in sleep, with her nose red from crying, she was lovely.

"Oh, the sweet girl," his mother whispered. "Pick her up, and let's tuck her into bed."

"She's likely to wake up." And likely to think he was taking liberties. Simon didn't relish the thought of being considered high and mighty *and* a rogue.

"Her legs are no doubt asleep with the rest of her. She'll have trouble walking anyway."

Simon gave a sigh and tapped Torey on the shoulder. When she didn't budge, he eased his arm behind her back, the other underneath her knees, and lifted her. She moaned softly and snuggled against him, her breath tickling his neck. Simon swallowed hard again as he ascended the stairs, Mother following along behind them, her hand on his back.

When they reached the hall just outside of her room, Torey roused and lifted her head from his shoulder. Her eyes widened as she met his gaze. "Am I dreaming?"

A chuckle lifted from Simon's chest. "No. I found you asleep in the library. Mother was afraid you might not be able to make it to your room after sitting on your legs for so long."

"Thank you," she whispered. "I—I think I can walk now."

"Of course." Simon set her down, his arms immediately missing the weight of her.

She stumbled, and he reached out to steady her, slipping his arm around her waist. She was tall enough to meet him face-to-face, and as he pulled her close, she gave a small intake of breath. "Thank you again," she murmured, her lips barely moving.

"My pleasure," he replied, unable to bring himself to look away from her gaze.

Mother cleared her throat. "Well, now. Let's get Torey settled into bed where she can stretch out and get the blood flowing to her legs again."

Simon released Torey slowly, to make sure she didn't stumble again. She stepped back and reached for her door. "I—I appreciate your help." She turned to Mrs. Crawford. "Both of you. But I'll be fine now."

Mother reached out and embraced Torey. "All right, my dear. Sleep well."

"Thank you. Good night to you both." She gave Simon one more shy glance and disappeared into her bedroom, closing the door behind her.

"Well," Mother said, her face lit with amusement.

Simon turned to her sharply and scowled.

Taking the hint, she shrugged. "Good night, then." With a chuckle, she walked down the hall.

Simon slid his hand gently along Torey's door as he walked by and headed toward his own room.

"Sleep well." His mother's words reverberated through his mind. He knew sleep wouldn't come easily tonight. New feelings were sprouting in his heart. Tenderness and longing such as he'd never felt toward a woman. He needed to think about them. Gain some perspective. He had only considered marrying young women of his own social status, though he'd never found anyone to hold his interest for long. He couldn't very well fall in love with a servant, could he? Or could he? There were no rules that indicated otherwise.

Perhaps, as Mother said, he just needed to get to know her better. He smiled as he reached his door. Yes, Mother was probably right. He would get to know Torey better. . .starting tomorrow.

ح

Amos narrowed his gaze and stared at the brute of a man standing on the other side of his desk. "Well?"

The man stared back, his cold eyes indifferent to Amos's growl. "No one has seen her in more than two weeks. Last anyone noticed, she was downtown, trying to find food and a place to stay. Thad Compton said you owe him two dollars, along with the rest of the money you owe him, for some fruit she stole from his man on the street. She stole from him more than once, and only the knowledge that she was your step-daughter kept him from alerting the police. He said if he'd known you were looking for her, he would have contacted you right away." The man gave a wicked grin. "But I think he was lying about that. He seemed pretty happy that she's causing you trouble."

Waving in irritation, Amos kicked his chair leg, sending the chair across the room. He didn't have time to worry about Thad Compton's pettiness. He had bigger problems than the paltry sum he owed the fruit seller.

He had to find the girl! "Where *is* she?"

"I'll find her."

"You'd better find her soon." Amos slammed his fist down on his desk, ignoring the pain shooting through his knuckles. "I don't have much time left."

Obviously not the slightest bit intimidated, the brute turned and headed toward the door. "I never fail."

Watching him go, Amos snarled. "You'd better not," he muttered, though the man was long gone. He stomped across the room, grabbed his chair, and brought it back to his desk. Piles of unpaid bills cluttered the mahogany desktop. A growl rose from within his chest. With a swipe of his hand he sent the bills flying.

If he didn't find that stepdaughter of his soon, he was ruined. The bank was threatening foreclosure on the house, and all of his accounts were months overdue. Mr. Shepherd was ready and more than willing to pay off all of the debts Amos had acquired and see that he was handsomely paid in addition. All Amos had to do was produce Torey. He knew the girl would rather die than do what he had planned for her, but that fact played little on his conscience when he considered what he had at stake.

Her virtue was a small price to pay for his life.

five

Torey awakened to the memory of Simon's arms holding her the night before. She giggled beneath the covers as imaginary butterflies fluttered about in her stomach. The look in his eyes had definitely shown more than merely interest in a dalliance, she'd wager. She smiled, then frowned as doubt sprang to life within her mind, choking out her pleasure at the possibility of Simon requesting to court her.

Or maybe he wasn't interested in anything more than a flirtation.

The smell of bacon wafting from the kitchen, directly below her room, beckoned to her stomach, inducing a growl. Mrs. Crawford insisted that Torey take Sunday breakfast in the kitchen with Simon, Mrs. Crawford, and Katherine. Torey would have enjoyed accompanying the three of them to church but thus far had stayed behind for fear one of Amos's acquaintances would be at the service and recognize her. She had confided that fact to Mrs. Crawford, and the woman seemed to understand, but Katherine voiced her disapproval each week. Simon seemed indifferent to whether she accompanied them to church services or not.

Today, more than ever before, Torey wished she could join them. Her new commitment still burned in her heart, and she longed to become part of a fellowship. Pushing back the covers, she released a sigh. Would her life ever be normal again? Or would she be looking over her shoulder for the rest of her days?

She washed and dressed quickly. After tidying her room and making her bed, she took the back stairs down to the kitchen.

"Good morning," Mrs. Crawford greeted her, a broad smile splitting her plump face.

"Good morning, Ma'am. Good morning, Katherine." Torey scanned the room, then relaxed. Simon wasn't there. She turned to Katherine, who lifted bacon from the iron skillet onto a platter. "May I help you?"

"Yes, thank you. Take this to the table." The housekeeper motioned to the platter. Torey did as she was bidden.

"Did you sleep well?" Mrs. Crawford lifted her coffee cup to her lips and glanced over the rim, awaiting Torey's response.

Torey felt the blush creeping to her cheeks. "Yes, Ma'am. I slept quite well. I'm sorry I fell asleep in the library."

"It's quite all right. I've been known to fall asleep during prayer myself from time to time."

A smile touched Torey's lips. "I didn't actually fall asleep during my prayer. . .more like afterward. I felt such peace that I suppose I just drifted off. I've never slept so deeply in my life."

"The peace of God passes all understanding." Mrs. Crawford's brow rose. "Do you mind telling me about it?"

Taking her seat, Torey smiled. "I found the Bible on the shelves when I was looking for a book to read. When I read about Jesus, it was like I'd never heard the story before, and I knew I had to pray and give myself to Him."

"Praise the Lord." Tears misted the woman's eyes.

Katherine plopped down a pan of muffins on the table. "Perhaps now you'll accompany us to services. After all, the Bible says we're to go to church. You may as well get started on the right foot."

"The Bible says that?" Taken aback, Torey looked to Mrs. Crawford to confirm or deny Katherine's statement.

"The Bible does encourage us not to forsake the assembling of ourselves together. But it doesn't necessarily say it's a sin not to go."

"I see. . ." The thought of wandering too far from the

Crawfords' home, especially to a public place where she might be recognized, didn't appeal to Torey at all. As a matter of fact, it terrified her.

"You don't have to go if you'd rather not. But we attend a small gathering not far from here. We'll take the carriage." She pressed Torey's hand and gave her a look that clearly stated she didn't believe anyone would recognize her.

"I'm not suitably outfitted for church services this week. But I will buy myself a proper dress from my wages and will attend with you next week, if that's agreeable."

"That's fine. We'll be pleased to have you accompany us."

From the stove, Katherine gave a "harrumph". "The Lord isn't concerned with our appearance, only with our heart."

"Which," Mrs. Crawford said firmly, "no one but the Lord is qualified to judge."

The housekeeper sniffed again but didn't reply.

"Good morning, ladies."

Torey's heart sped up at the sound of Simon's voice coming from the doorway behind her chair.

"Everything looks delicious, Katherine. I could smell your fine cooking all the way upstairs. I shaved so fast, I nearly slit my throat."

Obviously pleased with the praise, Katherine stood a little straighter and smiled broadly. "Sit down. Breakfast is almost ready."

"Thank you." Simon sat opposite Torey, and for the first time since entering the kitchen, he caught her eye and winked as Katherine set a platter of scrambled eggs on the table in front of him. He focused his attention on the elderly housekeeper. "How are you feeling this morning? We missed you yesterday."

Tenderness softened Katherine's features. "I'm much better. Thank you for asking."

Torey watched the exchange, still not sure what to make of

the wink. Simon had good qualities; anyone could see his mother's influence. He was thoughtful, a trait Torey had rarely witnessed in the men with whom she was acquainted. But just because a man was thoughtful to his mother and an aging housekeeper didn't mean he wasn't planning a flirtation with the maid. He caught her eye once more, and his smile sent waves of heat through her belly. "How are you this morning, Miss Mitchell?"

"Well, thank you."

"Able to walk without assistance?"

"Simon!" his mother scolded.

"It's all right, Mrs. Crawford," Torey said, determined not to let him see how his teasing affected her. After all, if he had felt even a percentage of the emotions she'd felt being so near to him last night, then she could imagine he must be confused by it as well. On the other hand, if he was a cad who only meant to play with her heart and then discard her when he tired of the game, then he had no right to tease her in such a manner.

If only she could know which instance best described his intentions toward her. She squared her shoulders. She couldn't very well come right out and ask about those intentions, but she could let him know that she would not be trifled with.

Katherine set a platter of fluffy biscuits on the table and took a seat. She folded her hands in front of her, elbows bent. She cleared her throat.

"Are we ready to say grace?" Mrs. Crawford asked, chuckling.

The aging housekeeper gave her a sheepish smile. "I didn't want breakfast to get cold."

"It's all right, Katherine. Of course we don't want your delicious food getting cold."

They bowed their heads, and Simon offered a prayer of thanks. Though the prayer was simple, Torey sensed Simon believed wholeheartedly in his words to God. Could a man with such faith trifle with a maid's emotions the way Amos seemed to enjoy doing at Beatrice's expense?

Simon said "amen" and raised his head. His brow rose in surprise as he caught her gaze across the table from him. He seemed to study her—a mix of bemused interest and possibly suspicion. Torey felt the heat in her cheeks as she realized she'd been caught watching him instead of properly bowing her head in prayer. Quickly she averted her gaze and studied the blue-flowered print on her plate.

Refusing to look at him, Torey remained silent during breakfast unless she was spoken to. Her relief knew no bounds when Mrs. Crawford pushed back her chair and stood. "I'd best go change for church."

"And I should as well," Katherine said, following her employer's example. The two women left the kitchen together.

Torey nearly panicked as she glanced at Simon's plate and noted much of his food still untouched. As though of their own volition, her eyes lifted, and she met his gaze. He smirked, and she rose quickly. Perhaps if she began cleaning up, he'd take the hint and get moving.

Unnerved, she reached for Mrs. Crawford's empty plate, but as she did so, she bumped her own glass, half full of milk. Desperately she tried to keep it upright, but it was too late. Despite her valiant attempt, the glass turned over, spilling its contents onto Mrs. Crawford's red-checked, Sunday morning tablecloth.

"Oh, no!" She grabbed a napkin and began to sop up the spill before it could spread to Simon's place at the table.

A warm hand covered hers.

She looked into Simon's gray eyes. "I'm sorry," she whispered.

His obvious compassion filled her with a longing to return her head to his chest where it had rested when she awoke last night.

"There's no harm done," he said. "The tablecloth soaked up the milk anyway."

He stood and picked up his plate.

Torey gasped. "Put that down!"

Startled, he practically dropped the plate back to the table. It clattered on top of silverware. "What's wrong?"

"That's my job."

His lips twitched beneath his handlebar moustache. "I assure you, I'm not trying to take it from you," he drawled.

"Of course not. But you shouldn't be doing housework. Besides, you haven't finished eating."

He lifted his plate again. "Katherine gives me twice what I can eat. I have to wait until she leaves the room to discard it so she isn't offended."

Torey smiled. She walked to his side of the table and held out her hand. "That explains the food still left on your plate, but the fact remains that I'll not have you doing my job. Please hand over the plate and allow me to clean up the kitchen."

Without waiting for him to comply, she grasped his plate, and he relinquished his hold.

"I, um, I wanted to thank you for your kindness last night, Mr. Crawford."

His Adam's apple bobbed in his throat, and Torey felt a strange bit of satisfaction that he seemed as disconcerted by the memory as she felt.

"Well, I couldn't very well leave you sleeping on the floor. You might have taken a cold."

"It was very thoughtful. I–I hope I wasn't too heavy." She cringed inwardly. What an utterly ridiculous thing to say!

Her stupidity apparently lessened his embarrassment, because he chuckled. "Are you doubting my manly strength?"

Eyes growing wide, Torey shook her head vehemently. "No, Sir. Nothing was further from my mind. I just. . .well, I am so much taller than most girls, I thought maybe you had

had a hard time carrying me." Her mind begged her to hush, before she made a complete fool of herself. Quickly, she turned and walked to the counter. She scraped his plate into the refuse pile and returned to the table.

He stayed rooted to his place, standing beside his chair, and she had to maneuver around him to gather the rest of the dirty dishes. He touched her arm, and Torey nearly dropped the stack onto the floor. Luckily, she composed herself just in time. "About last night, Miss Mitchell. . ."

Torey braced herself. Was this where the Lord of the Manor suggested an inappropriate flirtation, demanded one at the risk of the poor maid's position in the household? She squared her shoulders. "Actually, Mr. Crawford," she broke in before he could make his intentions known, "I wanted to discuss last night with you as well." She walked past him and set the stack of dishes in the sink. Then she turned and faced him once more.

"Yes?" His eyes narrowed, and he drew in a breath.

"Well, it's just that. . ." Words eluded her, and she fought to find something, anything to say that sounded firm and yet remained properly respectful of their individual places in the household. "Actually, Mr. Crawford, I just want it understood that I'm not the sort of girl a man such as yourself can trifle with. To be sure, I was caught off guard when I woke up and you were—well, you know where I was when I woke up—but that doesn't mean I am willing to compromise my morals."

"I see. . ." His gaze darkened, and Torey's heart raced as she envisioned an immediate dismissal. "So you thought I was so irresistibly drawn to you that I was going to insist upon an affair?"

"Well, I didn't think of it exactly like that, but yes."

He scowled. "I don't know what sort of men you are accustomed to, Miss Mitchell, but I was taught to be honorable—a lesson I learned well. Not only are my own morals far above mere dalliances, my walk with Christ means more to me than anything. I wouldn't compromise my relationship with Him for anyone—not even a pretty maid."

Mortified, Torey could only stare. Words fled her mind, and she couldn't utter a sound.

Obviously realizing he wasn't going to get a response from her, Simon inclined his head in farewell and strode past toward the kitchen door.

All the strength left Torey's legs, and she grabbed a chair, sitting before she fell in a heap to the ground.

She owed him an apology. But the thought of facing him again was nearly more than she could fathom. What if she just left? If she snuck out while they were at church, she'd never have to face him again. She thought of her meager savings: three weeks of wages she didn't deserve and had tried not to take but that Mrs. Crawford insisted upon paying her. She had enough to pay for a cheap room for a few nights. And perhaps she could find a domestic position, such as this one, somewhere before her money ran out. She knew enough about caring for a home now, that if she worked extra hard, a new employer shouldn't have any complaints.

She stood and walked back to the sink as unease crept through her. Leaving this home was a bad idea for more than one reason. Mrs. Crawford had insisted that she needed Torey because boarders would begin arriving anytime. Additionally, how could she even consider leaving after Mrs. Crawford had been so patient teaching her how to be a maid? And though she still wasn't the best maid in the world, she was finally beginning to hold her own.

She plunged her hands into the warm, soapy water and began to scrub the dishes. But her mind continued its list. The last reason she couldn't leave was because away from the security of this house, she would once again be all alone and vulnerable to Amos, should he be trying to find her.

At the thought of Amos, her pulse quickened and her

stomach knotted in fear. The door opened, and she turned suddenly, flinging sudsy water droplets to the floor.

"Whoa, take it easy," Simon said.

"I'm sorry. I thought you'd gone."

"Mother asked me to let you know we are headed to the church."

Torey nodded, still smarting from their earlier exchange. "Thank you for letting me know."

"You're welcome."

Torey swallowed hard. It was now or never. "Mr. Crawford. Please wait a moment." She dried her hands on her apron and walked across the room to where he stood, a wary expression on his face.

Gathering a deep breath, she forced herself to hold his gaze. "I would like to apologize for thinking the worst of you. You've never shown me inappropriate attention, and as you implied, I have no right to judge your intentions based upon the scoundrels I've known in the past."

His brow rose in interest, and Torey stepped back, an instinctive protective action. Why did she always have to say too much?

"Are you coming, Simon?" His mother's voice carried into the kitchen.

"Good day, Miss Mitchell." He smiled politely. "I accept your apology. Perhaps we've gotten off on the wrong foot."

"Perhaps," she replied, nearly weak with relief at Mrs. Crawford's timely interruption. She listened until the front door closed and she knew she was all alone in the house. In no time at all, she had the kitchen sparkling. With a satisfied smile, she decided to go upstairs and read her Bible. That was the least she could do, considering it was the Lord's Day and she had been unable to attend services.

A knock at the front door halted her ascent just as she reached the steps. She opened the door. A broad-shouldered man stood on the front steps, his face split into a friendly smile. He removed his bowler and pressed it to his chest.

"May I help you?" Torey asked, wishing she weren't alone in the house.

"Hello, Miss." His eyes darted to somewhere behind her. "Anyone else home?"

Every impulse in her screamed for her to lie, to say anything but the truth of the situation. But her heart wouldn't allow the sin—even in self-preservation. "I'm the maid," she replied. "My employers have gone to church, but they should be home shortly." There now, that much was true, depending on one's concept of time. Torey expected them to arrive back home within two hours. That was short compared to a whole day.

"Forgive my presumption, but I understand the owner of the house might be interested in taking in boarders."

"That's right." Torey started to relax. Mrs. Crawford hadn't advertised for boarders, insisting that God would send those He intended to take up residence there. But she'd spread the word at church and among their close friends. If this man was acquainted with someone associated with the Crawfords' circle of friends, then perhaps he was trustworthy.

"I wonder if I might take a look at a room? I am new to town, and I must admit my accommodations are less than acceptable. It would be a welcome relief if I were able to move in as soon as possible."

"I'm afraid I am in no position to allow a stranger into the house when the owners are away."

His cheery expression darkened but brightened again so quickly that Torey thought perhaps she had imagined the change in his demeanor. He gave her another attractive smile, showing beautifully attended, white teeth. "I am sorry to hear that. If I could only impose upon you to reconsider. You see, my time is up in my current room, and the landlord has already rented it to someone else. If I don't find somewhere to sleep tonight, I'll be on the street. I don't know if you can imagine such a thing, Miss, but the thought is less than appealing to me."

Torey's memory took her back to the two weeks she'd spent trying to snatch a few moments of sleep at a time, wondering whether she'd wake up and if she did, what would be awaiting her when she opened her eyes. The thought of this man enduring a night of such circumstances sent a wave of pity through her. She was about to welcome him in when a sudden thought came to her mind. Where was his bag? She looked into his eyes.

"Where are your bags, Sir?"

He scowled. "In my room, of course."

"But you just said your landlord has rented your room out. Surely he didn't steal your clothing. Unless you owed him rent."

The scowl deepened. "Are you suggesting I'm being dishonest?"

Torey's knees began to tremble as he took a step closer. "I wouldn't know, but I am afraid I must stand firm. You may not come in until my employers return from services. I am certain Mrs. Crawford would be happy to show you a room at that time."

His hand shot out, and he snatched her arm, his long fingers biting painfully into her soft flesh. "Like I said, Miss Mitchell, I want to come inside."

Torey gasped. Amos's thugs had found her! *Oh, dear Lord, help!*

As if by design, a loud bark filled the air just before a flash of brown, black, and white breezed past the stranger and shot inside the house.

"Abe!" Frank, the Nelson's gardener, followed him up to the house. "Beg your pardon, Miss," he said to Torey. "Mind if I hurry on inside and snag Abe before he destroys everything?"

"Be my guest," Torey said, standing aside.

The stranger's black eyes flashed in anger at his thwarted plan. "I'll be back," he whispered. "There's a certain man who wants you found."

"T–tell Amos I'm not going to the police. H–he can just leave me alone, and I won't tell a soul he killed that man at the theatre."

His brow rose. "Is that so? You're not going to tell anyone?"

Torey shook her head. "Amos has nothing to worry about. Tell him, and ask him to let me be."

A sinister smile curled his lips, and he turned and strode down the steps.

"Will you tell him?" Torey called after him.

His laughter followed him down the walk. "You can count on it."

six

Simon released a silent breath of relief when the preacher said the final "amen" and dismissed the service. It wasn't that the sermon was lacking or that it hadn't spoken to his heart. . .it had, but he felt uneasy leaving Torey home all alone after Frank had told him about the man standing outside their home. Yesterday, at least, Katherine had been upstairs and could have rousted herself had the man returned and threatened either of the women.

He fingered his moustache. For all he knew, the girl was in no danger from whoever had been lurking about the house. Perhaps she was an accomplice in a plot to harm or defraud him and his mother. Regardless, he didn't like the idea of leaving her alone. There were too many unknowns.

Tapping his foot, he waited in the carriage while his mother spoke at length with Reverend Graham. He eyed the pair, willing them to hurry.

"Stop fidgeting, Simon," Katherine admonished from her seat across from him. "You squirmed all during the preacher's sermon. I was ashamed of you."

Her outrage struck a humorous chord with Simon, but he tried to hide his smirk. "At my age, one would think I'd have learned to sit still in church."

"I completely agree. It's little enough the Lord asks of us to come and worship once a week with our fellow believers. The least you could do is pay attention."

"I'll do better next time." He smiled fondly at the housekeeper. "I promise."

She jerked her chin and stared out the carriage window.

"You needn't promise me. It's the Lord you should be worrying about offending. And don't think I don't know what you're up to, trying to hide your laughter behind that ridiculous moustache."

Simon forced himself to sober. The woman took her faith very seriously and had an enviable respect for the Lord. He'd wager she wouldn't allow herself to fidget in church if she had an ant crawling up her arm. "I'm sorry, Katherine. I have no business teasing you."

Fortunately for Simon, Katherine had never been able to stay annoyed at him for long. She gave him an indulgent smile. "I forgive you. Ah, here comes your mother."

Simon opened the carriage door and stepped out.

His mother smiled sweetly as he helped her onto her seat next to Katherine, then climbed in after her. "Thank you, Son." Mother sat heavily, trying to catch her breath. After adjusting her hat and smoothing her dress, she eyed Simon. "I told Reverend Graham that you want to hire someone to protect us—as though the angels of the Lord aren't encamped about us—and he said he'd keep a lookout for someone suitable."

"The angels may be hovering over the house, but they didn't keep Father from being killed, did they?"

Katherine and his mother gasped in unison. "Son, I know you have an ax to grind with the Lord right now, but I won't have you blaspheming."

"For shame," Katherine clucked. "You need to evaluate your relationship with God, young man. I don't think you're where you think you are."

Simon looked from one scowling woman to the other. He sighed. They were both more than likely correct. His father's death had taken a spiritual toll on him. He'd become cynical, if not bitter. No matter how hard he tried to shake it, he couldn't help but wonder what might have happened if God had allowed him to get back to the theatre booth a few moments sooner. Maybe he could have saved the man who had always been the foundation of his world.

Sometimes, going into his father's study at home sent waves of physical pain through Simon's chest, so great was his grief. Immersed in thought, he stared out the window, watching the cobblestone street roll past. The hypnotic effect combined with the *clip-clop* of the horse's hooves sent nostalgia through him. A longing clenched his chest—not only for his earthly father but also a longing for the closeness he'd once shared with his heavenly Father. Still, a part of him couldn't let go of the raging inside, the "why?" of it all.

Father shouldn't be dead. He had never hurt anyone and was known in life as a generous man. He gave without expecting anything in return. This hackney was proof of that. When their driver had approached Father with a desire to start a business hiring out his own carriage, Father had not only released the man from service but had also extended him a loan and sold him their carriage at a low rate. Then, rather than buying another carriage and hiring another driver, Father made a standing arrangement with their former driver and paid for a ride wherever he went— including the Sunday ventures to church.

Simon hadn't necessarily agreed with the arrangement, but when he'd voiced his concern over whether this was a sound financial decision, Father had bluntly told him that as a child of God he conducted personal business the way he believed God would. Those words had ended the argument before it had even begun. Father's steadfast belief that it was more blessed to give than to receive was a principle by which he lived his life.

Oh, how Simon missed him. He didn't want to blame God, but he knew in his heart that he did. And although he was willing to forgive, the feelings weren't there yet. He also knew that even if he renewed his trust in God, he could never forgive the man who had killed his father.

The memory of Father gasping for breath while he lay in Simon's arms haunted him. The dying man had taken a weak fistful of Simon's shirt and tried to pull him close. Simon leaned closer so he could hear. *"Giiieee. . ."* Puzzled, but unwilling to cause Father undue anxiety in the last seconds of life, Simon hadn't pressed for clarity. He'd simply smiled through tears and kissed his father's hand, assuring him.

The longer Simon thought about the incident over the next few days, the more he convinced himself that his father was saying, "Get him." So he'd made a decision that he would look for the killer for the rest of his life if he had to. The man would get what he had coming.

"Looks like Abe got loose again." Mother's amused voice brought Simon back from his memories.

Katherine grunted. "That dog is a menace. He should be locked up."

Simon glanced out the window as the carriage pulled to a stop in front of the wrought-iron gate. Frank held Abe firmly by his collar and spoke to Torey. Simon frowned. Was it his imagination, or did Torey appear to be distressed?

Simon exited first and helped the ladies from the carriage; then he paid the driver and headed up the walk.

Frank darted a gaze to him. Was that a nervous look?

Simon focused on Torey. Her face was drained of color, making her wide violet eyes even more pronounced.

"What's going on here?" he demanded. "What's happened?"

"My fault, I'm afraid," Frank said quickly. A little too quickly? "Abe escaped again. I reckon I didn't get his pen locked when I fed him this morning. Before I knew it, he dashed out and headed right over here." He scratched his balding head with arthritic fingers. "Can't imagine why ol' Abe loves this place so much. Shot right through the house and into the kitchen just like he knew where he was headed."

Katherine sniffed. "Any dog with even a little sense can

smell a chicken roasting in the oven." She scowled at the gardener and stomped past. "You should train him to stay home!"

Watching the exchange hadn't deterred Simon one bit. Up close, he could see that Torey trembled. This was more than the dog running into the house. "What else happened?"

Torey shot a glance at Frank, her wide eyes speaking volumes to him. And for some reason, Frank forsook his loyalty to Simon—loyalty built of years of acquaintanceship. He shrugged. "Reckon that's all I'm at liberty to say. I best get this animal back home."

"And I need to help Katherine prepare lunch." Torey took off before Simon could detain her and demand answers.

He let out a frustrated grunt and watched her scramble up the front steps and disappear into the house.

Something wasn't as it seemed with that girl, and he had every intention of discovering what was going on in his household. In the meantime, he planned to devote as much of his day tomorrow as necessary to securing a guard for the house.

❧

Torey barely made it through lunch without losing every bite she forced down. Her overwrought nerves threatened to snap any second. She kept a tight rein on her emotions, not allowing the tears that welled up in unguarded moments.

Thankfully, Frank had agreed to her plea not to tell Simon about the hired thug. It had taken some convincing before he would believe the Crawfords were in no danger from the man—only she was at risk. She'd finally persuaded him that she alone was the target, and if she thought for one moment Simon or Mrs. Crawford—and yes, even Katherine—were in any danger, she'd immediately confide in Simon. For some blessed reason, Frank had agreed.

"Torey dear, are you feeling poorly?"

Torey looked up from her plate to find Mrs. Crawford studying her, a frown of concern creasing her brow.

"Perhaps a—a little. May I be excused? If you will notify me when you're all finished eating, I'll come back down and clean up."

"You'll do nothing of the kind," she replied firmly. "Go and get into bed. You've most likely caught the same thing that ailed poor Katherine yesterday."

Nearly weak with relief to have the convenient excuse, Torey nodded. She stood and scraped her plate into the refuse pile. "Thank you. If you'll excuse me now, I'll be in my room lying down."

Thus far, Torey had avoided Simon's gaze, fearful of what she might discover in the depths of his eyes. But as though drawn of their own volition, her eyes looked at him. Just as she'd feared, he studied her, suspicion clouding every feature. His expression veiled an admonition not to bring trouble to their household. She averted her gaze immediately.

"I'll be up to check on you later, Torey dear."

"Thank you." Barely able to contain the tears choking her voice, Torey couldn't say anything else. She knew that when the woman came to her room, it would be the last time they saw one another. Torey couldn't take a chance that Amos might harm one hair on Mrs. Crawford's precious head. As much as she wanted to, she couldn't stay in this lovely home.

Dragging her legs up the steps to her room, she forced herself to consider what might happen if she didn't go away. Her mind spun with planning her departure, though her heart nearly broke at the thought.

She had no choice but to keep the dress she wore, as the one she had arrived in had long since been burned. But she would leave money on the nightstand to pay for it. The rest of her savings should last for a few days if she spent frugally and found another position as quickly as possible.

Or perhaps she should spend part of her meager funds and purchase a train ticket to someplace where she could make a fresh start. New York City, maybe? Amos would never find her there, and as large as that city was, she shouldn't have too much trouble finding a suitable position.

She stretched out on her bed, knowing she had to wait until at least six. If she left earlier than dusk, she ran the risk of someone observing her departure. Then she'd be forced to admit Amos was looking for her. Or rather that he'd found her.

Mrs. Crawford had her reasons for not informing Simon that Torey had run away from home or why, and Torey wanted to respect her wishes. Besides, she wasn't thrilled with the idea of making Simon privy to the information in the first place. He would probably consider her an accomplice and would want to take her to the police.

Torey closed her eyes. From experience she knew she'd better sleep as much as possible now. If she couldn't find a place to sleep tonight, she wouldn't sleep at all.

Only five hours remained until dusk. Tears slipped from the corners of her eyes, soaking into the hair at her temples and dampening her pillow.

Five hours before she left this wonderful place behind for good.

۞

Sweat beaded on Amos's forehead. His jaw dropped open, and he stared unbelievingly into John Shepherd's smug, wrinkled face. He wanted to ask the old man to repeat what he'd just said, but he knew he would hear the same thing again.

"I can see by the look on your face I'm right." The scrawny, nearly toothless man stared hard, his eyes glittering like onyx. "This changes the dynamics of our relationship quite a bit. Wouldn't you say?"

"B—but how did you find out? No one knows but. . ." His eyes widened.

Mr. Shepherd cackled. The "apes" to his right and left

chuckled on cue. "It seems I'm more adept at finding those I'm looking for than you are."

"You mean, you've been looking for Torey?" If the old coot had found the girl, he had no reason to honor their agreement. Amos was as good as dead. He glanced at the apes and could feel their meaty fingers around his neck, squeezing the life from him.

Amos swallowed the bile rising in his throat and inwardly kicked himself for not being more forceful about finding her, even if it had meant combing the streets himself.

"I know precisely where she is." Mr. Shepherd leaned forward in his brown leather wing chair. "Now, I have an amendment to our original agreement. Sit down and let's talk."

Eyeing the man warily, Amos did as he was bidden. He preferred to stand, but one didn't remain on his feet when John Shepherd commanded otherwise.

"If you know where my stepdaughter is, then I assume you have no intention of honoring our agreement?"

Mr. Graham gave him a look of mock indignation. "Of course I intend to keep my end of the bargain. I will honor all of your debts and pay you handsomely—when you deliver the girl to me."

"But if you already know where she is. . ."

"Yes, but I am not a kidnapper. I have decided I need someone to accompany me to events. Someone beautiful and completely devoted to me. Your job is to convince the lovely Victoria to come to me willingly. I do not want a slave. I am too old to put up with an unhappy woman in my home. I have discovered life is much easier if a man keeps his woman happy. You may think me foolish, but I am ready to invest in a mutually beneficial relationship with your stepdaughter."

Taken aback, Amos could only stare. He'd known for some time the old fool was enamored of Torey. And who wouldn't be? She'd always been polite to the old man, and he'd soaked up every smile. He'd watched her like a hawk, growing fonder of her as she grew older. Why hadn't Amos initiated a financial arrangement earlier? He inwardly kicked himself at his oversight.

Shepherd grinned. "I can see you doubt my sincerity."

"Oh, no, Sir! I'm just not quite sure I understand. Are you offering Torey marriage?"

"Perhaps, eventually. For now, I am offering her security and protection. She'll have anything she wants as long as she keeps me happy."

"And you think my ability to deliver her willingly to you is worth your silence about the man I killed?"

"You would do well to accept my generous offer. Convince the girl that my proposal is in her best interest, and you will have no worries. Unlike you, I keep my word."

Heat seared Amos's neck and ears. Oh, how he wished he could throw John Shepherd's offer in his face, but he knew he had no choice. Not only did he have to get time alone with Torey, he had to convince her that her reputation and virtue were worth a life with this shriveled old fiend sitting across the desk from him. It wasn't going to be easy. But what choice did he have?

He drew in a quick breath and nodded. "All right. Where is she?"

seven

Torey squared her shoulders and opened the window. Thankfully, her childhood days spent at Grandmother's, trying to prove to the boys next door that she could do anything they could do, wouldn't be wasted. The ancient oak tree outside her window provided the perfect ladder for her to shinny down.

Capturing her bottom lip between her teeth, she closed her eyes and tried not to imagine what landing on the ground would feel like should she miss a step.

Dizziness swept over her as she looked at the oak she would have to reach. Unfortunately, no amount of time spent climbing trees as a girl had removed her dreadful fear of heights. It took every ounce of willpower not to back out and return to bed. But Amos's thug could return at any moment. And he might consider it worth harming the Crawfords to get to her.

The thought bolstered her courage. Carefully, she stepped onto the awning outside her window and forced herself not to look down. She inched toward the tree, balancing on the sloping canopy. She caught hold of a limb hanging close to her. With caution, she stepped across to a V in the trunk.

One branch at a time. She could do this. She had to do this.

Hanging onto a fat limb for dear life, she stepped down to the next V in the mighty oak. The back door opened below her. She looked down and froze. Simon stood on the porch, staring out at the pinkish blue sky as the sun said its final farewell before disappearing altogether into the dark of night.

Oh, God. Make him go back inside. I can't stay up here like this much longer.

But God chose not to answer her flung-up prayer. Simon stepped off the porch and walked to the gazebo twenty feet behind the house. As she watched him, Torey momentarily forgot her fear of heights and her angst over Simon's presence preventing her from climbing down. He sat on a bench inside the covering and bent forward at the waist. Resting his elbows on his knees, he raked his fingers through his hair. Torey caught her breath at his troubled demeanor. She longed to go to him and offer to listen if he needed someone to confide in, but to do so would reveal that she was running away. Then she might not have the courage to go through with it.

After a few moments, Torey's hands began to hurt from hanging onto the branch. Her legs trembled from her precarious position, but she didn't dare move to a more stable limb for fear of alerting Simon.

More agonizing minutes passed, but rather than go back into the house, Simon stayed in-his position. Torey assumed he was communing with the Lord. She didn't have the courage to ask God to make him stop, so she tightened her grip and prayed for strength.

A twig beneath the tree snapped, startling Torey. She glanced down, and her stomach twisted with dread. A man stood below her, staring in the direction of the gazebo. A gasp escaped her throat as the shadowy figure walked slowly toward Simon.

Broad-shouldered and extremely tall, the man could very well be the same thug who had threatened her just that morning. Her throat tightened, and she began to scramble down the branches, mindless of the danger. When she reached the ground, she found her voice. "Simon!" she called, running as fast as she could toward the man. "Look out!" She barreled toward the would-be attacker and knocked into him with the full force of her weight. He stumbled forward, enough for Simon to recover and jump to his feet.

"What is this?" Simon demanded.

"I saw him coming after you," Torey said, trying to catch her breath.

"Who are you, Mister?"

"Reverend Graham sent me."

Torey gasped as she realized this wasn't the same man who had almost kidnapped her earlier.

"Why didn't you go to the front door?"

"A man like me doesn't knock on the front door, Sir."

For the first time Torey realized he was a Negro. He could have knocked on the Crawfords' front door. But how was he to know that?

She stepped forward. "I made a mistake, Mr. Crawford. From the tree, he looked liked someone else." Turning to the man, she extended her hand. "I apologize for trying to knock you over."

A grin split his face. "Never hardly felt it, Ma'am."

"What is your name?" Simon asked.

"Nathaniel Wright. Folks just call me Nat."

Simon stepped forward. "Why did the reverend send you to us, Nat?"

"Says you might have a job for me."

"I'm afraid we don't have any positions available. We've no need for a driver, as we have no carriage."

Nat twisted his hat in his hands. "Reverend says I might make a good bodyguard because I'm so big."

"Oh." Simon seemed at a loss for words. He recovered quickly. "Let's go inside and we can talk about your credentials."

"I don't know what 'credentials' is," Nat replied. "But I'd be happy to talk about it."

Torey smothered a grin. Perhaps if Simon and Mrs. Crawford hired Nat, she wouldn't have to worry about Amos and his thugs. Maybe she could stay after all.

Simon led the way to the house, then held the door, motioning the massive man into the house ahead of him.

When Torey walked by, he leaned toward her. "Later, we'll discuss what you were doing in the tree."

She swallowed hard and nodded. Once inside, she excused herself and headed for the kitchen door.

"Miss Mitchell," Simon asked, "will you please find my mother and ask her to join me in the kitchen?"

As she knew she would, Torey found Mrs. Crawford in the library, reading. The woman glanced up, and a smile lit her face. "Oh, wonderful. You're up. How are you feeling?"

Torey felt heat rising to her cheeks. "I'm much better. Thank you."

"Praise the Lord. Would you care to join me?"

"Simon—Mr. Crawford, that is—asks that you join him in the kitchen."

A frown creased her brow, but she set down her book. "Did he say why?"

It wasn't really her place to tell Mrs. Crawford about Nat, but Torey saw no reason not to share what she knew, since she'd been directly asked.

"A man showed up outside. He says the reverend sent him over to be your bodyguard."

Instant joy brightened the woman's face like the electric lights Torey had seen at the Hammonds' Christmas ball last year. The woman lifted her arms. "Oh, precious Lord. Thank You for watching over us and sending exactly the people You have prepared to be a part of this household."

She winked at Torey. "Prayers of the children of God are powerful when we pray according to His will."

Torey smiled. "Yes, Ma'am."

"I'd better go greet my new bodyguard." Her lips twitched as she passed. "I wonder what Simon will have to say about God answering my prayer. He wanted to hire a boxer." She shook her head. "Can you imagine someone choosing to get the stuffing beaten out of him?"

"I imagine a person would have to be pretty desperate."

"I suppose. But I have to question his intelligence a little. Do you want to join me in the kitchen? You didn't have your supper. Katherine wrapped some chicken left over from lunch into the icebox. You could fix yourself a sandwich. The ice is nearly all melted, but the chicken should stay cold enough until Mr. Jackson brings the ice wagon around tomorrow."

Loathe to face Simon again so soon, Torey shook her head. "I think I'll just go back to bed."

"All right, Dear. Good night."

Torey watched her go. With a sigh, she climbed the steps to her room. Once there, she flopped, fully clothed, onto her stomach on the soft bed. She rested her chin in her palm. Now what should she do? She'd slept almost all day in anticipation of a sleepless night, so she was wide awake.

A loud rumble twisted her stomach—protesting the many hours that had passed since she'd eaten a decent meal. Her mind wandered to the chicken, wrapped up and waiting in the icebox. A meal completely out of her reach for now—until she was sure Simon had retired for the night. She couldn't run the risk that he might see her and demand an answer as to why she had been hiding in the tree in the first place.

If only she'd known at the time that the man was no threat, she could have kept quiet and followed through with her plan. On the other hand, a part of her was ever so grateful that her departure had been thwarted. And with Nat hired to protect the house and Mrs. Crawford, maybe Amos would realize it would be better to leave her alone. After all, she'd given her promise of silence. She would keep that promise, if he would just leave her alone and let her build a new life with the Crawfords.

Again, her stomach protested its emptiness. She tried to focus her mind on something else but found herself coming back to the chicken. As soon as she heard Simon close his bedroom door, she was going to go downstairs and fill her aching stomach.

❧

Simon hesitated by Torey's door. A soft glow shone onto the hallway floor from her room. For a moment he was tempted to knock and demand his answers, but he thought better of it. After her accusation that morning, he didn't want to do anything that smacked of impropriety. He picked up his pace once more and went into his own room.

He knew he'd sleep a little easier tonight with Nat downstairs in the small room off the kitchen—the same space that had once been the driver's quarters. Mother had offered the new bodyguard a room on the same floor as the family, but Nat had politely declined, his expression clearly stating his shock that she would even suggest such a thing.

Simon chuckled. The bodyguard would become accustomed to Mother's complete lack of snobbery and social propriety. And even if he never became accustomed to it, he would at least become less taken aback by it.

At first he had been reluctant about hiring the man, but Mother reminded Simon of their bargain. He had promised to give God until tomorrow morning. So after verifying that the good reverend had indeed sent the man, Simon hired him. With a grin, Simon stretched out on his bed without removing his shoes. He knew when he'd been bested. God had sent a bodyguard.

Simon only hoped God would soon send boarders to cover the cost of adding a maid and a man to keep watch over the house and its occupants. He knew from examining their financial records that Father had provided well for them, but how could he have known of his untimely demise? If he had, he might not have spent most of his life savings to add a wing to the house, which he insisted was necessary for when Georgia and her growing family came for extended visits.

Whether Mother had agreed with his decision or not would go with her to the grave. Simon knew that. Now she said simply that God's purpose was for Father to build the wing, not for Georgia, but to bring in boarders who needed help— whether physical or spiritual. Perhaps she was right. And if so, he hoped God would begin sending them soon.

Simon's musings ground to a halt at the sound of a creaking board in the hall just beyond his bedroom door. He shot up and tiptoed across the floor. Cracking the door enough so that he could look out, he saw just the bottom of a dress— the same dress Torey had worn earlier that evening.

Indignation shot through him. After all they'd done for her, she was going to sneak out in the night without so much as giving her notice? Or maybe she was up to something else. Like thievery. Perhaps she intended to steal and get out now that Nat was employed.

After he was sure she'd gone down the back steps, he slipped out and followed, dread clenching his chest. One way or another, he intended to confront her about why she was in the tree earlier. The odd occurrence didn't go very far to reinforce his confidence in her.

Tiptoeing down the steps, he took great pains with his boots, making sure they didn't make noise and alert Torey to his presence. At the bottom of the steps, he frowned. She had turned and gone into the kitchen. The only thing of value in the kitchen was the silver service. Only a not-so-smart thief would go after such booty in a room close to the guard. Especially when Torey knew there were jewels and antiques in other sections of the house.

Alarm seized him as he watched her grab a knife and head across the kitchen—right toward Nat's room. In a flash, he pushed open door. She spun around and the knife hit the ground with a clatter. Moving quickly, Simon reached the weapon before she could retrieve it.

"Simon! You nearly scared the life out of me." She clutched at the high neckline of her shirtwaist gown.

Shaking the knife in her direction, Simon snorted. "Looks like I came down just in time." He tossed the would-be weapon onto the counter and stayed between it and Torey.

"I was only going to take a little. Y—your mother said Katherine put it up for me."

Trying to wrap his mind around this information, Simon frowned. "My mother told you to take the silver?"

"The silver?" She stared at him as though he had lost his mind. The second that realization dawned on her face, Simon knew he'd made a gargantuan mistake.

"You thought. . ." As though all her strength had left, Torey wilted into the first chair she could grab. "What did you think I was going to do with the knife? Kill Nat so he wouldn't stand in my way? It just so happens I was hungry. Your mother told me Katherine had wrapped the rest of the chicken and placed it in the icebox."

Before Simon could respond, Nat appeared at the doorway of his room. "Is everything all right, Mr. Crawford?"

"Yes, Nat." Simon waved him away. "Sorry to disturb you."

"No need to apologize. That's what I'm here for," the bodyguard answered, then closed his door once more.

Disappointment at his own stupidity clutched Simon's gut. What real reason did he have for suspecting Torey of foul play? She might not be very good at her job, but that wasn't a criminal act. He was on the verge of apologizing when he suddenly remembered that he did have a reason. "What were you doing in the tree earlier?" he demanded.

"Stealing silver," she retorted, anger flashing in her eyes. "Didn't you hear it clacking in my pockets?"

"Very funny." Simon refused to be swayed by her sarcasm. "Now the real reason."

"Can't I just like climbing trees?"

"You have to admit it's an odd thing to do."

A shrug lifted her shoulders. "That depends on your perspective. Little boys climb trees all the time, and no one thinks anything of it."

He had to chuckle at her logic. Still. . . "That may be, Miss Mitchell, but I'll surmise you are not the kind of girl who climbs trees for fun. Let's try again. What were you doing?"

"Oh, all right. I was climbing out to sneak away." She scowled at him. "Are you happy now? I suppose you'll tell your mother."

Simon stepped forward and seized her by the arm, lifting her to her feet. He studied her startled face. "Who were you sneaking out to meet? An accomplice?"

"Y—you think I'm an accomplice? I haven't done anything wrong." The anger was gone from her voice and in its place came a pleading for him to trust her. "I would never hurt your mother, Mr. Crawford. Never in a million years."

Simon wanted to believe her. Looking into her beautiful eyes, now wide with fright, he couldn't imagine her capable of deceit. Her lips, parted and glistening, drew him, and so help him, he wanted to kiss her.

"Simon Crawford, unhand that girl this instant!"

The spell broken, Simon turned and caught the full force of his mother's outraged glare. He released Torey.

"Now, what on earth is going on here?"

"Ask her," Simon said, refusing to apologize for trying to keep his mother safe. Perhaps he'd been wrong in this instance, but the girl still hadn't provided an answer about why she was lurking in the tree. As far as Simon was concerned, she was under suspicion until she did. No matter how beautiful her eyes or sensual her lips. No matter how deep her dimples or pleasing her figure. There were too many unanswered questions about this girl. And until someone made him privy to whatever facts his mother seemed to

know about Torey, he wasn't going to let down his guard—
not again, anyway.

Mother shifted her gaze to the girl, her eyes alight with
curiosity.

A sweet sigh escaped Torey's full, rosy lips. Simon glanced
away.

"I was leaving, Mrs. Crawford. I was afraid you might not
let me go if I told you my intentions, so I decided to sneak
out." Heat rose to Torey's cheeks as she realized how silly her
next statement was going to sound. "I'm afraid I climbed
down the tree outside my window."

"I see." Mother's expression held no anger, no judgment,
nothing that would make Simon believe she thought it odd
the girl would climb a tree and risk breaking her neck to
leave a home where she'd been taken in, cared for, given a
job, and practically treated like one of the family.

Whether Simon liked it or not, that was his mother's
nature. If she decided God had sent someone to her for help,
she wasn't going to turn her out because of something like
this. Instead, she walked across the room and cupped Torey's
face in her hands. "And what changed your mind?"

"I—I saw Nat and thought he was going to. . ." She
shrugged. "It doesn't matter. I've decided to stay."

"Do you need to talk?" Mother asked. "Has something
happened?"

"I—" She darted a gaze toward Simon.

He scowled but took the hint. "All right, I'm going." He
stalked to the door.

Only when he reached his room and stretched back out on
his bed did he realize something that should have occurred
to him earlier. Torey had been prepared to run away tonight.
She had given up her plans in order to protect him. Was that
the mark of a woman who was out to harm him and his
mother? The answer filled his heart. *No.* What had she said?

"I would never do anything to hurt your mother. Never in a million years."

The tenderness filling his chest confused him. Torey confused him. He thought of her, downstairs with his mother, most likely pouring out her heart. But about what? What had happened to cause her to want to run away?

Releasing a frustrated breath, he closed his eyes. Perhaps tomorrow would bring the answers he sought.

eight

Torey's heart leaped in her throat as the hackney neared the bank where Simon worked. Mrs. Crawford had insisted Torey take the day off to buy herself a suitable outfit for church. Over Torey's protests, the woman had also insisted upon Nat accompanying her. Torey was sure Simon would be furious when he discovered that the newly hired bodyguard was protecting her instead of his mother. In order to hurry back to the house, she had entered the first dress shop in sight and purchased the first gown that looked like a decent fit. Much to the salesgirl's chagrin, Torey had waved away the suggested hat, shoes, and handbag.

She could have gone to town and back much more quickly if not for Mrs. Crawford's request that she stop by Simon's bank and deliver his forgotten lunch.

As the carriage slowed down, she glanced out the window. A sense of familiarity fluttered over her as she stared at the brick building. The pewter plaque on the outside of the bank boasted SAVINGS AND LOAN in gold lettering. She'd been here before.

Searching her mind, she recalled waiting in the carriage while Amos went inside to conduct business just days before that fateful night at the theatre. Torey shuddered, pushing the vivid images from her mind. No matter how hard she tried, she couldn't completely push back thoughts of that poor man Amos had killed. The memories were never far away.

The carriage came to a complete stop, and Nat hopped down from the driver's seat where he sat next to the driver. He opened the door. "We're here, Miss Torey."

Torey gathered a deep, steadying breath, snatched the basket with Simon's lunch from the seat next to her, and stepped out.

"Don't you worry none, little girl," Nat said. "I'll be standing right here, watching you like a hawk. Anyone bothers you, I'll come running lickety-split."

Tenderness filled Torey. She smiled at the giant of a man. Even with her height, she had to look way up to meet his gaze. He had no way of knowing that she felt completely safe with him. It was Simon she dreaded facing.

"Thank you, Nat. You've no idea how that eases my mind."

The black man beamed with pleasure.

Anxiety seized Torey as she reached the door to the bank. Resisting the urge to run back to the carriage and thus force Simon to go hungry until supper, she pulled on the handle and went inside.

The bank bustled with people. Smartly dressed men and women clerks stood behind counters, conducting business with equally well-dressed men and women customers.

Torey scanned the room. In one section of the bank behind a swinging gate sat several wooden desks. She peered closer, recognizing the area as the place Mrs. Crawford had told her she'd find Simon. Squaring her shoulders, she clutched the basket tightly in an effort to still her trembling hands and forced her legs to move forward.

Her heart skipped a beat. She located him sitting at the third desk on the left side of the area behind the swinging gate. Intently studying documents on his desk, Simon had failed to notice her. Wishing he'd look up, Torey stood still for a moment until a man walked toward her and paused, obviously needing to get around her. Her cheeks warmed. She smiled her apology and stepped through the gate.

Simon looked up as she approached his desk. His brows rose in surprise, and he stood quickly, nearly tipping over his chair. He raked his hand through his thick, dark hair. "Miss Mitchell!

What brings you downtown?" He leaned in closer and lowered his voice. "Does my mother know you've come?"

Torey scowled. "Well, I certainly didn't take it upon myself to deliver your lunch. Don't worry, I'm headed straight home." She slammed the basket onto his desk and spun around to leave.

"Wait." Simon caught her by the arm, gently nudging her back around to face him. "I'm sorry. Forgive me?"

The little-boy appeal of an unruly lock of hair across his forehead combined with the pleading in his gray eyes softened Torey. She gave him an indulgent smile. "I forgive you."

A look of relief slid over his face. He smiled. "Did Mother really send you all the way here just to deliver my lunch?"

"I–I was coming to town anyway. To, well, to purchase a suitable outfit for Sunday services. But you needn't worry; I'll work late to make up the time."

"I'm not worried about the time. That's between you and my mother. Look, since you're here anyway, why don't you allow me to treat you to lunch? There is a wonderful little establishment just around the corner. They have an Irish cook who makes the best corned beef and cabbage I've ever eaten."

"What about your lunch?" Torey pointed toward the basket.

A smiled twitched Simon's moustache. He lifted the lid and peeked inside. "The chicken sandwich you never got to eat last night." Mischief gleamed in his eyes as he caught her gaze. "I'd rather have the corned beef. Katherine never has to know."

Torey felt torn. A part of her ached to spend the time alone with him—as long as he continued to display this charming side of his character. The other side of her realized the danger of allowing herself to grow any fonder of him. She didn't want to lose her heart to a man whose station in life was higher than hers.

Obviously recognizing her hesitation, Simon cocked his head to the side. "The only thing in life more enjoyable than discovering a wonderful restaurant is sharing it with someone."

She knew he exaggerated. Lifting an eyebrow, she showed her skepticism.

"All right," he said, that boyish grin nearly her undoing as he switched tactics. "Allow me to make up for my heretofore inexcusable manners."

No one could doubt his sincerity. Torey felt her resolve weaken and crash. She smiled. "All right. I'd enjoy it."

His face lit with pleasure. "Just let me grab my jacket, and I'll be right with you."

He grabbed the basket and walked a few feet before stopping beside another desk, where a man worked diligently. Simon cleared his throat to gain his attention. "Robert, I'm about to escort this lovely lady to lunch. Would you care to take this off my hands so that it doesn't go to waste?"

"I don't understand," the man replied. Torey noticed his shirt, though pressed and clean, was worn thin. His face was gaunt, and she realized nourishing meals were more than likely few and far between.

"This lady brought my lunch all the way downtown, but I'd rather treat her to Mahoney's around the corner. You'd be helping me out if you'd take this off my hands."

"Why, I suppose I can do that for you," the man replied. "Thank you."

"I should thank you. If you didn't take it, I'd be forced to forego my engagement or be wasteful."

The man eyed the basket hungrily, and Torey could almost feel the aching in his stomach. Compassion filled her. How could a man work in a bank and not have enough food to sustain him?

She watched Simon walk across the room. Another man stopped him and held out a stack of papers. Simon took them and glanced back to Torey. He smiled and held up one finger to indicate he would just be a moment. Torey smiled back. Feeling conspicuous in the middle of the bank, she motioned to him that she would wait for him by the door. He nodded his understanding, then returned his attention to his work.

Torey stood watching the comings and goings with interest. How Simon must enjoy such a position. He appeared to be efficient, and she could imagine that someday he would be a very important man. Unease gnawed her at the thought. How long would he be interested in the likes of her?

"Miss Mitchell? How lovely to see you."

Torey jerked her head and gasped at the sight of John Shepherd, friend and partner of Amos. Dread clenched her gut, and her heart began to race.

"M—Mr. Shepherd," she stammered. "I—it's a pleasure to see you again as well, Sir."

His gaze slid over her, and Torey had the uncomfortable sense that he was looking at her as hungrily as Robert had eyed the chicken sandwich Simon had offered him. The old lecher slid his tongue over his thin lips and smiled a nearly toothless grin. Torey fought to keep from shuddering in revulsion.

"What brings you into town?" the old man asked.

"I'm, um. . ." Torey darted her gaze back to Simon, but he was too busy to notice.

"Does your stepfather know you're all the way down here unescorted?" he asked in such a manner that Torey might have considered his concern grandfatherly, had he not just skimmed her figure again.

"N—no, he doesn't know." Attempting a smile, Torey realized he must not have been in touch with Amos these past weeks, or he would more than likely know she had run away. How could she have been so foolish as to come to the business district?

"Well, your secret is safe with me, my dear."

"Oh, thank you, Mr. Shepherd. I am ever so grateful."

"My pleasure." He hesitated a moment as if considering his thoughts. Panic rose inside of Torey at his next words. "It would be an even greater pleasure if you would allow me to escort you to a fine lunch and then home."

"Oh, no, Sir. I—"

"Ready, Miss Mitchell?"

Torey nearly fainted in relief as Simon approached.

"Yes. I'm ready," she said, aware that her voice sounded breathless. She had to get them out of there before Mr. Shepherd discovered she was working for Simon or before Simon discovered she was well acquainted with Mr. Shepherd and heard Amos's name brought into the conversation.

Mr. Shepherd's brows rose, and anger flashed in his eyes. "I see you are otherwise engaged," he said, his voice dangerously low.

"Yes, Sir. I am sorry." She smiled, careful to show her dimples. "Perhaps another time? You've no idea how I appreciate your thoughtfulness."

"Are you going to introduce us, Miss Mitchell?" Simon's tone was hard-edged. Torey wasn't sure if it was a natural response to Mr. Shepherd's obvious animosity or if the incident reopened his suspicions.

Without giving her an opportunity to make the introductions, Simon extended his arm. "Simon Crawford."

Recognition shone in Mr. Shepherd's squinty eyes. "Your father was George Crawford?"

"Yes, Sir. You knew my father?"

"I did. A good man. I was sorry to hear of his death. The bank hasn't been the same these past few weeks."

"Thank you." Simon shifted his feet, and Torey sensed his discomfort.

She watched the exchange with interest. She knew Mrs. Crawford was a widow, but she'd had no idea the loss was so recent.

"If you'll excuse us, Sir," Simon said. "I promised to take Miss Mitchell to lunch."

Mr. Shepherd's thin lips curved in a smile, but his gaze held Torey fast. His hard expression revealed his displeasure with the situation. Confusion wafted over Torey's mind. Why should he care if she went to lunch with Simon? Perhaps he *did* know that she'd run away and Amos had offered a reward for her return. Had the old man intended to kidnap her, take her home, and collect the bounty? A shiver slid up her spine. She forced a smile. "Good day, Mr. Shepherd. It was a pleasure to see you again."

"I assure you, the pleasure of seeing your pretty face again has brought me immeasurable joy." Before she could protest, he snatched her hand and brought it to his wet lips. It took every ounce of willpower she possessed to keep from jerking away and wiping the back of her hand on her skirt. But she contained herself as he walked away, followed by two of the largest men she had ever seen except for Nat.

Simon scowled. "Shall we go, Miss Mitchell?"

Torey's heart crashed. Gone were the pleasant tones of their earlier conversation. His voice had reverted to the cold suspicion to which she'd grown accustomed.

"No, thank you, Mr. Crawford. I've decided to return to your mother so that Nat can look after her."

Alarm flashed in his eyes. "Do you mean to tell me that Nat came along with you instead of remaining home?"

Jerking her chin, Torey narrowed her gaze. "At your mother's insistence. I'd have just as soon come alone."

"Come on," he commanded, taking her by the arm and escorting her from the bank. He stopped at the carriage and handed the driver some bills. "Paul, please take Nat home. Come to Mahoney's around the corner in about an hour, and I will escort Miss Mitchell home at that time."

"Yes, Sir."

"Wait." Nat stepped forward, determination flashing in his dark eyes. "Those wasn't my orders. Miz Crawford told me I was to look after Miss Mitchell until she returned home."

Simon's moustache twitched. "Don't you think she'll be safe with me?"

Nervously, Nat twisted his hat between his massive hands. "Well, now. I didn't exactly say that. . ."

Patting the man on the arm, Simon gave him a reassuring smile. "Trust me. I won't let anything happen to Miss Mitchell. She's much too valuable to our household."

Indignation shot through Torey, and she attempted to jerk away her arm. A chuckle lifted from Simon's chest, and he held her fast.

Glowering, Torey sent him the full force of her glare. How dare he insult her! Perhaps Nat didn't recognize the sarcasm, but she certainly did. Valuable indeed! They both knew she was worthless as a maid.

"That be what you're wanting to do, Miss Mitchell?" Nat studied her intently, awaiting her answer.

Suddenly Torey didn't know what she wanted. Part of her wanted to bolt, to jump into the carriage and return home to her room and her position as a hireling. Away from Simon's intoxicating presence, teasing, and out-and-out suspicious nature. But the side of her that was beginning to believe Simon was wonderful forced her to remain silent. She nodded.

She knew by Simon's intake of breath that he was just as surprised by her answer as she was. He loosened his grip on her arm. "Go on home, Nat. I promise to take good care of Miss Mitchell. I'd appreciate your making sure my mother is safe."

"Yes, Sir. You got nothing to worry about."

The black man climbed up next to the driver, and the carriage rolled away.

Torey stared after it, unable to find her voice, unable to meet Simon's gaze.

"Come on. I promised you lunch."

"Yes, Sir," she murmured.

"Please, don't call me *sir* anymore. I feel extremely old when you do so."

"Yes, Mr. Crawford." Nearly grinning over his reference to being old, she purposely kept her gaze riveted on the walk in front of her.

"I'd prefer if you'd call me Simon. I believe we know each other well enough for first-name usage, don't you?"

"No, I don't." Finding her courage, Torey glanced at him as he opened the restaurant door for her. They stepped inside. Torey's stomach protested its emptiness as heavenly smells of pepper and beef reached her nostrils.

Simon escorted her to an empty table and held her seat. When he was seated across from her, he studied her intently. "Now, why don't you think we know each other well enough to use first names?"

Torey's gaze darted to the serving girl walking toward them. The woman grinned broadly. "Why, hello, Mr. Crawford. Back again? And you've brought your young lady with you."

The pretty brunette sent him a cheeky grin. Then she turned sparkling brown eyes on Torey. "And I'd say he's chosen well."

Heat suffused Torey's cheeks. "N–no, I'm not. . .I'm just. . ."

"Lizzie, meet Torey Mitchell. Miss Mitchell works as a maid at my mother's soon-to-be-full boardinghouse."

"Oh, I see." Mischief sparked in her eyes, but she kept her thoughts to herself as she looked from Torey and back to Simon. "What'll it be for you today, Sir?"

"Two plates of corned beef and cabbage. I promised Miss Mitchell here the best lunch in town."

"And he's not exaggerating, Miss."

"Thank you," Torey replied, relaxing a bit under the girl's warmth.

"So, *Miss Mitchell*," Simon began when Lizzie walked

away, "you don't believe we know each other well enough for first names."

"No. I believe we've been acquainted long enough, and you are more than free to call me by name. But my position in your household makes it impossible for me to do the same." She fingered the blue gingham tablecloth and forced herself to look him in the eye to show him how serious she was. "It isn't proper. I shouldn't even be here with you. Did you see how the serving girl looked at me when she discovered I'm your mother's maid?"

"All she said was, 'I see.' " Simon shrugged. "How could you read anything into that?"

"Honestly. Her tone of voice implied that she believes we are courting at best, and at worst. . ."

"At worst?" he urged.

Releasing a heavy sigh, Torey wished she'd never raised the issue. But now she was sure he'd never let it go. "At worst she believes we are carrying on an. . ." She hedged a moment, searching for an appropriate, yet inoffensive word. "An improper relationship."

His face reddened. "Oh. Are you sure that's what she thinks?"

Torey nodded. "Women have a sense about what other women are thinking."

"I apologize, Miss Mitchell. It never occurred to me that inviting you to lunch might cause your reputation harm."

Torey couldn't help the warmth seeping through her chest at his concern. This was the side of Simon that she knew she was falling in love with. The side that had carried her up the stairs, saved her from the dog, examined her burns.

"It's all right, Mr. Crawford. I assure you the damage is minimal." She smiled to show him her utter lack of concern at the moment.

Lizzie returned before he could respond. She carried two steaming plates and set them down.

"Enjoy," she said with a wink and a grin.

"Wait, Lizzie." Simon reached out and stopped her by gently touching her arm before she could walk away.

"Need something else, Mr. Crawford?"

"No. This is fine. I just. . .I think I may have given you the wrong impression of my relationship with Miss Mitchell."

Eyes widening, Lizzie shook her head. "I didn't think anything, Mr. Crawford."

"It's all right," Simon gently assured her. "I just don't want you to think there is anything between myself and Miss Mitchell. She came to town to deliver lunch to me, and I offered to treat her to lunch instead, to return her kindness."

The girl's brow creased. "So you took her to lunch to thank her for bringing you lunch?"

Torey couldn't suppress a giggle. When the girl put it that way, Simon's explanation sounded like he was trying to hide the real reason for their luncheon. "Mr. Crawford found a two-day-old cold chicken sandwich less appealing than this wonderful-smelling meal. So he used his gratitude toward me as an excuse to forego the lunch I brought from home and to come here instead."

The confusion left Lizzie's face, and in its place, understanding dawned. "Well, now, that makes sense. Why didn't you just say so in the first place? Mr. Crawford will do anything for some of Mrs. O'Roark's corned beef and cabbage."

Simon grinned. "Yes, Ma'am."

"I'll leave you to it," Lizzie replied, and with a final wink at Torey, she sauntered away.

Resting his elbows on the table, Simon folded his hands. "I'd like to say the blessing."

Torey followed his example, lacing her fingers in front of her. She closed her eyes and listened to his deep, rich voice while he thanked the Lord for their food. Remembering the man at the bank who'd accepted Simon's lunch, she thanked God doubly for her portion.

After Simon said "amen", Torey looked up at him. "Mr. Crawford? The man at the bank. . ."

"I was going to ask how you knew Mr. Shepherd."

Inwardly, Torey cringed. She should have been more specific to begin with. "A—actually, I was referring to the other man. The one you gave your lunch to."

"Oh, yes. Robert. Do you know him too?"

"No, I do not, and please don't be sarcastic. Mr. Shepherd was a business associate of my stepfather's. I've known him for several years. I don't care for him, but I couldn't very well have been rude." She sniffed and shot him a pointed look. "Like you're being."

"I apologize for my rudeness, Miss Mitchell." He studied her face. "But surely you understand why I find it difficult to trust you when you refuse to tell me where you came from and why you showed up outside our window filthy and half-starved."

"Your mother knows the truth."

"So she claims."

"I didn't lie to her." Torey felt the old indignation rising. She was on the verge of mentioning that his own mother had insisted she keep her story private and not share it with Simon for now. But she knew that might be a source of contention between them. Better to let him believe she was the one who wanted to keep things secret.

"I assure you, Mr. Crawford, that I have my reasons for keeping my privacy. But I can also promise that you will be informed eventually. Please try to trust me for now. You have nothing to fear from me. I have given my word I will not hurt your mother."

Releasing a heavy sigh, he nodded. "I suppose I have no choice but to try to believe you are being honest."

"Yes."

"All right. What about Robert?"

Making the mental shift in topic, Torey nodded. "Have you noticed how hungry he is?"

A troubled frown creased his brow. "Yes. He is raising his brother's five children. His salary at the bank doesn't stretch far when he has to feed and clothe his nieces and nephews."

"Where are the children's parents?"

"Apparently, their mother became ill and died very suddenly. His brother tried to hang on for his children's sakes, but he was all but destroyed without his wife. One morning, he simply brought the children to Robert and dropped them off. He left and never returned."

"How tragic." Compassion caused an ache in Torey's heart.

"Yes, it is. Robert works at the bank by day and delivers ice by night. But it still isn't enough. He rents a couple of rooms in a tenement. The prices are outrageous. And as you can see by his thinness, he'd rather do without than deprive the children of one bite. But there's only so much a man's pride can take, and I've been trying to figure out a way to help without insulting him."

An idea swished inside Torey's mind. "How much do you think your mother would charge him for a couple of rooms?"

Simon frowned. "Are you serious? He is taking care of *five* children. Children who would be left at the house while Robert is working."

Torey shrugged. "Do you really think your mother would rather see a man half starving than to endure a little inconvenience? Besides, how healthy can it be for children to live in a rat-infested tenement building? It would be much better for them to live in a clean environment where they can run and play outside each day."

Simon scowled and pushed away his plate. He leaned back in his chair and squinted. "You know, Miss Mitchell, you remind me a great deal of my mother."

Torey wasn't sure if the statement was meant to be a compliment or not, but she couldn't help but smile. "Thank you, Mr. Crawford. No one's ever given me such high praise."

With a defeated grin, he shook his head.

Torey savored a bite of the delicious meal. She felt a sense of satisfaction that God had a hand in this day's events. And the thought came to her that things were about to get interesting at the Crawfords' home.

nine

"Shh! You're going to wake Mr. Crawford."

Simon's ears perked up at the sound of loud whispering coming from the hallway outside his door. He groaned. Six o'clock on a Saturday morning. Why did children always wake up at the crack of dawn? The five children and Robert had been living at the boardinghouse for three days, and life as Simon knew it had changed forever.

"Hurry up and take him into the girls' room." More scuffling and whispering ensued.

"Okay, but keep the shirt tied around his mouth so he can't bark."

Simon frowned and sat up. *Bark?* Whose shirt?

"Hold onto him!" The panicked voice rose above a whisper.

"I'm trying!" All attempts at quiet were halted.

A scream rocked the house.

"Get him!"

"Hurry, he's running away!"

Simon shot from his bed, stripped off his nightclothes, threw on a pair of trousers, and shrugged into a shirt. Still fastening buttons, he hurried barefoot to the door and flung it open.

"Stop!"

Four sets of feet skidded to a halt.

"Turn around."

They complied, and four pairs of guilt-ridden eyes stared back at him.

"What's going on here?" he demanded.

The youngest of Robert's clan, a three-year-old girl named

Sarah, screamed and ducked for cover behind her twelve-year-old brother, Mike. Simon focused his attention on the oldest boy. "Well?"

The boy swallowed hard and stared at the hallway floor.

Crash!

Another scream—this time coming from downstairs—demanded Simon's attention. Without waiting for an answer, Simon made a run for it, skipping as many steps as he dared on the way down. All four children followed, whooping and hollering at the top of their lungs.

"Let go, you filthy beast!"

A groan erupted from Simon. Not again! He followed the sounds of outraged shouting through the kitchen, where Katherine, shaking in anger, swept up a broken crock of sugar. She scowled and pointed to the back door, which had been propped open as Katherine tended to do each morning in order to "air out the house." No matter that it was downright chilly outside.

Simon ran through the kitchen but stopped short of exiting the house as his gaze scanned the yard, halting at the clothesline where, once again, Abe and Torey engaged in a game of tug-of-war with a freshly washed sheet.

Trying to hide his smile, Simon watched the determined set of Torey's jaw. He knew she had learned that the dog wasn't to be feared. The hairy beast only wanted to have a little fun. Unfortunately for poor Abe, Torey didn't appear in the mood to provide the dog his moment of entertainment. He playfully growled, pulling so hard his back legs slipped out from under him. Recovering, he kept his grip. The children cheered him on.

"Turn it loose!" shouted Torey. Her eyes flashed as she yanked hard, pulling Abe with her. Simon's brows rose. All the hard work she had been doing had definitely paid off by increasing her strength.

Deciding to put an end to her struggle, Simon stepped off

the porch and walked barefoot on the frost-covered grass until he reached Torey and the dog. He gripped Abe's collar. Prying the sheet from the dog's mouth, Simon handed it to Torey. She scowled. "Honestly, Simon. If you don't encourage your neighbors to keep their dog locked inside a pen that he cannot get out of. . ." Her voice trailed off, but he caught the gist of her meaning.

"I know," Simon replied, attempting to sound duly compassionate to her plight.

"Hey, you can't take that dog." Mike stepped forward, assuming command with a fierce scowl.

"Yeah!" Bolstered by their brother's courage, the eight-year-old twins, Toby and Tommy, followed Mike's lead, and each took a step forward, careful to stay behind their brave older brother. Pale-faced even with angry red splotches dotting their faces, the children looked as though a stiff wind might knock over the biggest among them. Hardly intimidating.

Simon finished tying the sheet through the dog's collar then straightened. "Sorry, he has to go back to his owner."

"He's ours," Toby asserted.

"Yeah," Tommy supported, finding the courage to step all the way up to Abe. He knelt and slung his arm across the dog's shoulders and neck, pulling the animal close for a hug. "We found you, didn't we, Boy?"

Abe responded with a long, wet lick, jaw to forehead. Tommy gave a gleeful laugh. "See?"

"Listen, children," Simon said. "I hate to tell you this, but you didn't find this dog; he found you. He gets loose and runs down here at least three or four times a week."

Feeling a tug on his shirttail—which had remained untucked in his haste to dress—he glanced down at little Sarah. Her bottom lip puckered and trembled.

Simon kept a firm hold on Abe and hunkered down to the child's level. "What is it, Sweetheart?"

"Pwease don't take our dog," she whispered, her beautiful blue eyes filling with tears. "We wuv it."

Behind him, Simon heard Torey's soft intake of breath and what he was sure was an "ahhh" coming from her.

He swallowed hard, wishing for all he was worth that Abe belonged to him so he could make a present of the ornery animal to the children. But a fact was a fact. The dog belonged to the Nelsons, whether they ignored him or not, and no amount of tears would change that. He reached out and pulled a strand of white blond hair from the girl's wet cheek and tucked it behind her ear. "Sweetheart, I wish I could let Abe stay, but he's not my dog."

"Yeah! He's ours."

"You're stealing him!" The twins gave him identical glares.

"Shut up," Mike growled at the boys. "He ain't stealing nothing. The stupid dog already has a family."

"Hey, you said we could keep it!" Tommy hollered, still hanging on to Abe.

"Yeah, you promised." Toby stomped over to his brother until they were barely an inch apart. He took on a "tough guy" stance and pushed out his chest. "I oughtta pound you for being a big fat liar, just like Pa!"

Mike's hand shot out, and he grasped a handful of the boy's shirt, nearly lifting him off the ground. "Take it back."

"I ain't gonna! It's true. You look like him and act like him." His sneer deepened. "You even smell like him."

Before Simon could process the situation, Torey stepped forward. Gently, she covered Mike's hand. "Please let go, Michael. Hurting your brother isn't going to solve anything."

"Mind your own business, Lady," Toby sneered. "You ain't our ma! You ain't nothing but a maid."

Incensed, Simon stepped forward, leading the dog. Torey glanced at him and shook her head. "I know I'm a maid," she said to the children. "But that doesn't mean I don't know what it's like to be disappointed. I lost both of my parents too. Just like you did. But you can't allow anger to control your life. I know losing Abe is a big disappointment. But that isn't a good excuse to take out your anger on others." She focused on Mike. "You're bigger than Toby. If you take your hand to this little boy, you'll hurt him. Do you really want to do that? It seems to me that you really want to protect him—"

"Hey! Who you callin' a little boy, Lady?" Toby snarled.

"Shut up." Mike released him abruptly, and the boy stumbled back but gained his balance short of hitting the ground.

"Mike! Leave Toby be!" All attention turned to the kitchen door where the oldest child, thirteen-year-old Melissa, stood, her face flustered. She flew down the back steps and stopped in front of Mike. "What did you do? What's happened here?" She glanced around at the four guilty faces, then turned her gaze to Simon. "I'm so sorry if they've caused you any trouble. I'll take them upstairs immediately."

Torey stepped forward. "It's all right, Melissa. The children thought Abe was a stray, when really he's just a menace who refuses to stay in his own yard." She shot the dog a glare that would have wilted the strongest of men. But encouraged by the attention, Abe wagged his tail and *woofed* happily, despite his restraint. Merry peals of laughter rose up from the children.

A helpless grin curved Torey's lips. She shrugged and sighed heavily, shaking her head in exasperation. Simon threw back his head and laughed. He'd had no idea how infectious the sound of children's laughter could be. *What would it be like if Torey and I were parents to these children? Or any children? Our own flesh and blood?* He met her gaze, and to his surprise, she held it, her cheeks blooming with color. Was she thinking the same thing? A wave of heat hit his stomach full force, and his legs and arms lost strength.

"Abe!" The Nelsons' long-suffering gardener hurried down the path that separated the Crawfords' house from the house next door. "This dog is going to be the death of me," he puffed. "Any damage this time? Or did I get here before he could destroy anything?" He scowled at the dog. Undaunted, Abe wagged his tail and took advantage of Simon's slackened grip. He jumped up on Frank, his wet paws imprinting the front of the gardener's shirt.

The children laughed uproariously at the dog's antics. Simon shrugged and gave Frank a sheepish grin. "Sorry, I was distracted, and he broke loose from me."

In the midst of the chaos, Katherine appeared at the doorway. "If you're going to make such a racket, I'll be forced to close the door." She looked at Frank and sniffed.

He smiled, taking off his hat. "Morning, Ma'am. I'm sorry to disturb you, but you know ol' Abe here. He can't stay away from the place."

"Well, he broke the sugar crock. You ought to teach him some manners. Or give him some attention so he's not always running off!" She scanned the group. "Too bad the Nelson children are all grown and gone. If you ask me, what that dog needs is a bunch of boys and a little girl to play with." She turned and stalked back inside, letting the door bang shut behind her.

Simon looked to Torey, whose lips twitched. Her beautiful eyes glinted in amusement. Katherine might act like a grouchy old woman, but inside she had a heart of gold. And she had a point. The dog and the children needed each other.

The children had grown silent, as though they were afraid to believe in the dream that Katherine had just ignited.

"What do you think, Frank? Should I talk to Mr. Nelson about Abe coming over to play?"

Nothing could have stopped the onslaught of pleas as the children talked over one another, stating all the reasons they should be allowed to play with him. Frank visibly melted when little Sarah tugged on his sleeve. He looked down. "Yes?"

"Pwease wet the puppy come over. We wuv him."

Frank cleared his throat. "Well, now. Course, I'm gonna have to talk it over with my boss. He's not crazy about the dog anyway. Bought it for his grandson to play with during visits— that was when his son lived here in Chicago. But not long after they got ol' Abe here, the boy up and moved his family to San Francisco. Now Mr. Nelson is stuck with the animal."

Toby stepped forward. "You know, we could take real good care of Abe. We could wash him and brush him. Feed him and give him water."

"I want to put ribbons in his hair!" Sarah said, stroking the dog's fur.

Tommy gave her a withering look. "He's a boy." As if that settled the matter.

She jerked her chin stubbornly and continued stroking the dog's ears. "He wikes ribbons." Abe flopped onto his stomach. Resting his head between his paws, he sighed and closed his eyes, clearly relishing the attention.

"You ain't putting no frilly, girly stuff in the dog's hair, and that's final!" Toby said, taking up his brother's righteous cause.

"I can so. Can't I, Mr. Simon?" She turned her wide blue eyes on him, and Simon knew he was a goner.

"Well. . ." He turned to Torey for support.

A delightful laugh blew from between her lips. She glanced from the scowling twins to the glaring Sarah. "That's an argument for another day. How about if we let Mr. Frank take Abe back home while we go clean up for breakfast?"

Groans of protest hit the air.

"Now, listen up." Simon stepped forward and tried to sound firm. "No disobedience or no dog. Is that clear?"

"We ain't gonna get it anyway," Mike said glumly, walking past Abe without even glancing the dog's way. "We never get nothin'."

"Oh, Mike." Melissa shook her head and followed him to

the steps. "We've never lived in such a nice place either, but we do now," she said with wisdom and patience far too mature for her thirteen years of age. She cast a hopeful glance at the dog. "Maybe things are changing."

Simon couldn't help the stinging behind his eyes. He looked away quickly so no one would see, but as he turned, he caught Torey's own misty-eyed gaze.

God had most definitely ordained their lunch meeting earlier in the week so that Torey could get through Simon's thick-headed lack of vision about such matters. These children needed a home, decent food, spiritual input. People to take an interest in them. So far, Mother was delighted with the children. She insisted upon reading them a story each night. First a chapter from the Bible and then a fairy tale. The children relished the attention—even the boys, who'd stopped pretending indifference almost immediately.

After all the children had entered the house, Simon stayed back and allowed Torey to go first, carrying her empty clothes basket.

When they entered the house, Mother was just coming through the inside kitchen door. "Good morning, everyone," she greeted. "Are everyone's hands washed for breakfast?"

The children rose and headed for the sink. Katherine pumped water onto their hands while they scrubbed.

A frown creased Mother's brow as she glanced at Torey. "Have you already begun laundry?"

"Yes, Ma'am." She leaned closer and dropped the volume of her voice. "You mentioned taking the children on an outing today, but I wanted to finish my washing first."

Following Torey's example, Mother kept her tone low so the children couldn't hear what was being said. "I meant for you and Simon to take the children. I planned to stay home and do the washing."

"Oh, no—"

"What?" Simon cut off Torey's protests. "What do you mean I'm taking the children on an outing? What about Robert?"

"Mr. Cole works all day at the bank and half the night delivering ice. He's sleeping, and I'm not waking him up. He needs his rest. Have a little compassion," she admonished.

Heat burned Simon's ears. When she put things in that perspective, he supposed he was being rather selfish.

"All right. Where are we going?"

"A day in the country will do the children good."

"Don't you think it's a bit chilly for that?" He glanced at the poorly dressed children. "They aren't properly outfitted for this sort of weather."

"I suppose you're right." She gave a sharp nod. "All right. They can go to the country next Saturday. Today, a nice trip downtown. Buy them two outfits each. Something to wear to school and outside for play, and something to wear to church. New shoes and coats. And treat them to lunch in the hotel restaurant."

"Mother, I hate to point this out, but the purpose of a boardinghouse is to make money. I think you're losing money in this arrangement."

She waved away his protest. "Simon, you have a lot to learn about the ways of God. Don't you remember what your father always said? We must conduct our financial affairs according to what we believe Jesus would do. What do you think Jesus would have us do for these children? Turn away from them? Let them all catch pneumonia?"

"No, of course not. I didn't say we shouldn't buy them some clothes. Just that perhaps you should pray about a couple of boarders who can afford to pay full rate."

"You let the Lord and me worry about that." She looked him over and frowned. "You're not wearing any shoes, your hair isn't combed, and your shirt isn't tucked in. What are you doing?"

"Ask them," he replied, jerking his head toward the children, who were filtering back to the table.

Simon excused himself to go upstairs and finish dressing. He thought of the five children awaiting a decent meal in the kitchen. Children without a father. Just like him. No, not like him. These children were abandoned. His father was taken from him. Frustration welled up. The police had made no progress in the search for his father's killer. They seemed to have chalked the whole thing up to a robbery gone wrong, as though that explained their inability to locate the killer. Simon lathered cream over his face and took his razor from his nightstand. He examined his reflection in the mirror and made a silent promise. *I will find the man who killed Father. And he will pay for what he's done.*

Almost immediately he heard another voice inside of him. *"Forgive. . ."*

Simon shook away the voice, pushing past the conviction. He'd be ready to release the anger and hatred once the man responsible was brought to justice. And not before.

❧

Amos's hand shook as he read the letter from John Shepherd that had arrived just that morning. The old bully hadn't bothered to show up in person this time. Instead he'd sent one of the apes to do his bidding. Amos looked past the polite greeting and reread the body of the letter:

> *A young lady of mutual interest to us has been seen keeping company with Simon Crawford, son of the late president of the Savings and Loan. I am sure you can understand how this ironic twist of events might cause problems for us both. I'd advise you to make haste in performing your part of our agreement.*
>
> *Sincerely,*
> *John Shepherd*

Amos wadded up the paper and tossed it aside. What work of fate was trifling with him? Torey had taken up with Simon Crawford, of all people?

The cloud of frustration gave way to a ray of hope as an idea came to him. Perhaps this turn of events could be used to his advantage. Particularly if the girl had feelings for the young man.

He chuckled. He could always find a way to make things work to his advantage. And this case was a prime example.

The time had come to let the girl know she couldn't run from him and get away with it. He glanced down at some writing on a slip of paper on his desk. The address where Torey was living. By the end of the day, she'd be back in his home, and all his problems would come to an end.

ten

A chill wind whipped around Torey's ankles as she stepped outside to remove the clothes from the line. She'd made a deal with Mrs. Crawford that morning before leaving to take the children on their outing. Torey would accompany Simon only if Mrs. Crawford promised not to touch the rest of the laundry. With great reluctance, the woman had agreed. So now at nine o'clock, when everyone inside was going to bed, Torey was getting the last of the clothes off the line.

A few snowflakes blew, melting as soon as they settled on the ground. The presence of the first flakes of the year reminded Torey how good God had been to her. What if she'd never seen Mrs. Crawford praying through the window? More than likely, she'd be somewhere alone in the dark and cold—somewhere fighting for survival.

Apprehension slithered up Torey's spine. She shuddered and quickly tossed a shirt into the basket, then reached for the next. Until a couple of months ago, she'd never been afraid of the dark. Now, she dreaded nightfall. She never knew what danger lurked in the shadows, and her imagination tended to run away with her.

In order to calm her quivering insides, Torey began to sing: "Blessed assurance, Jesus is mine. . . ." Was that a twig snapping? Torey jerked her chin, then closed her eyes in relief as she scanned the yard and found no one. "O what a foretaste of glory divine."

Snap. She stopped. That was definitely a twig. Heart racing, she stood paralyzed with fear, not daring to turn around.

Snap. "What luck to find you outside." Dread hit Torey's

stomach, knocking the breath from her. That mocking voice could only belong to one person.

Torey's heart crashed to her toes. Her chest rose and fell in a defeated sigh. She turned. "Amos."

He stood, barely discernable in the starless, moonless night. "You've been a very naughty girl," he whispered.

"Please, Amos. Just leave me alone."

"I'm afraid I can't do that. There is too much at stake."

"I told your man last week that I wasn't going to make a fuss. I'm good for my word. Just leave me alone. I've made a new life for myself. I'm happy."

"Doing menial labor?" he chuckled. "That's hardly what a girl like you was made for."

"I like working for the Crawfords."

"The Crawfords?" He snickered. "Perhaps I've underestimated you."

Not understanding but definitely offended by his insinuating tone, Torey frowned. "What do you mean?"

"Oh, come now. A girl with your looks content with being a maid?"

"I don't know what looks have to do with happiness, but I am very content with my position."

"And what of Simon Crawford? No designs on him?"

"Simon? How do you know him?"

"Ah, so it is true."

"What?" Wishing he'd stop being so evasive, Torey fought the urge to scream.

"I've heard on good authority that you've been keeping time with the young Mr. Crawford."

Torey gasped. "That's not true. I'm simply a hired servant in this household. And whoever told you otherwise is sadly mistaken or flat-out lying. Mr. Crawford has no interest in me beyond a servant-employer relationship."

"I'll just bet."

Indignation darted through her. "Don't judge everyone by your own low morals. Simon is a Christian and a gentleman."

"Ah, I see you do hold him in high regard." He waved away her protest before it could be voiced. "Regardless, your feelings for him won't matter. You're coming home with me immediately. I have plans for you, or have you forgotten?"

He reached forward and snatched her arm.

"No!"

"Keep your voice down," he snarled.

"I'm not going with you." Torey's voice was surprisingly steady. "If you attempt to kidnap me, I'll scream. And if that doesn't work, I'll run away at the earliest opportunity."

"Make no mistake. You *are* coming home with me. And you won't run away." He stood over her, his sneering face close enough for her to smell the after-dinner brandy on his breath. "Do you want to know why you won't run away or attempt to call out?"

His fingers bit painfully into her arm, and her bravado crumbled. "W–why?"

"Because. . ."

The back door opened, and much to Torey's relief, Nat appeared. "Miss Torey?"

With a muttered profanity, Amos released her arm and disappeared behind the gazebo.

"Yes, Nat?" Torey's voice trembled.

"Miz Crawford asked me to come and see about you. Says it's taking too long to bring in the clothes. Says she's worried about you."

"I'm sorry. I'll hurry."

"I'll help."

Oh, Lord Jesus, thank You for Your hand of protection.

"Thank you, Nat." Cringing at the poorly attempted lilt in her voice, Torey quickly pulled the rest of the clothing from the line. "You can carry the basket."

Once safely inside the kitchen, Torey's legs refused to hold her. The room spun, and she heard Nat's concerned voice just before he dropped the basket and lunged for her.

Then there was only darkness.

ꙮ

Simon paced the hall outside Torey's bedroom door, wishing the doctor would come out and tell him what was wrong with her. If he'd had any doubts that he was beginning to care for her as a man cares for a woman, this episode had erased them. He wanted to be in there, holding her hand, feeling the pulse beating beneath the delicate skin on the underside of her wrist, and knowing she was going to live.

The door opened, and Mother walked out. Simon hustled to her. "Well? How is she?"

"She'll be fine. The doctor said it was a simple faint. Smelling salts brought her right around."

Relief flooded Simon's chest. He leaned against the wall. "Thank the Lord."

"Yes." Mother gave him a knowing smile. "You're in love with her?"

Heat crept up Simon's neck. "Don't make it more than it is for now."

"But you admit you care for her."

Unable to resist a grin, Simon nodded. He felt giddy inside just admitting such a thing. "I've never felt this way about a young lady before."

"You couldn't do any better than Torey."

"If I could only be sure. Sometimes, I can forget that there are things I don't know about her—things like, why was she wandering around the city half-starved the night I found her outside our window?" He raked his fingers through his hair. "But at other times, I worry about her reasons for being here. What if it's just a little more than coincidence that she showed up a mere two weeks after Father's death?"

"Hogwash."

"Sometimes I agree, and I consider myself a suspicious fool for even thinking it about her. But at other times. . ." He shrugged. "I just don't know."

Mother reached forward and patted him. "Son, I know your father's death hit you hard. But you have to learn to trust people again. Remember, just a week ago, Torey knelt in our library and asked the Lord to cleanse her. She repented of anything she's ever done, and God made her a new creature in Christ Jesus."

"Are you trying to tell me something?"

"No, I'm asking, how would you feel if she were somehow close to your father's death?"

"I'd feel like she deserves prison!" What was Mother getting at? She knew something about Torey. Surely this wasn't it.

She held up her hand. "I assure you, Torey had nothing to do with it. But until you're willing to look beyond what she may have been before you met her, you're not ready to truly love her for the woman she is today."

The door opened again before Simon could respond to his mother's remark. Dr. Everson smiled. "Your maid will be fine."

"What caused her to faint?" Simon asked.

"She had herself a good scare, that's all." His eyes squinted in amusement. "You might want to let her do her work during the day and let her stay inside at night from now on. I think she has a healthy fear of the dark. Asked me to leave her light burning."

"Thank you," Simon said, feeling foolish that he'd been so worried. "We'll remember that."

The doctor gave him a knowing wink and handed him a bottle of smelling salts. "You might keep these on hand just in case she faints again. She's still a little shaky."

"Honestly, Davis Everson, don't tease my son. You'll scare him away from the first girl he's shown any real interest in."

Mother clucked her tongue at the ornery doctor. She held out her hand. "Simon, give me the salts."

With a scowl, Simon handed them over. "Thank you for coming, Doctor. Mother will see you out."

Needing to be alone with his thoughts, Simon went to his room and sat wearily on his bed. He leaned forward, resting his elbows on his knee. A knock at his door brought him upright. "Come in."

The door opened, and Nat stood at the threshold, his gaze darting from the floor to Simon and back to the floor. "I'm sorry to disturb you, Sir."

Simon stood. "Not at all. Please, come in." He motioned to a chair next to his desk. "What can I do for you?"

"It's about Miss Torey."

"What do you mean?" Simon's defenses alerted.

"I seen her talking to someone outside when I opened the door. I couldn't hear what she was saying, but she sounded real scared."

Alarm swept through Simon. "Where did the person she was talking to go?"

A shrug lifted his massive shoulders. "I don't see so well in the dark, Sir. I just seen him take off, lickety-split. And poor Miss Torey finished up as fast as her little fingers could work. I reckon she was so scared she up and fainted."

Simon considered the new information for a minute. "Nat, I am giving you another assignment. I'll be happy to pay you more, but in addition to keeping an eye on my mother, I'd like you to look after Miss Mitchell."

"What if your ma sends her off again, like she did the other day when she took your lunch? I can't be in two places at one time."

"Don't worry about that. I intend to discuss this with my mother. She'll be made aware of the very real danger Miss Mitchell might be in." He reached out his hand, and Nat took it in a bone-crushing shake. "I believe I can convince her to cooperate given these circumstances."

"I think it's real good you want to protect Miss Torey," Nat said softly. "Some folks need more looking after than others."

Clearing his throat, Simon searched Nat's face for evidence the man was insinuating Simon might have special feelings for the girl. He didn't need the entire household privy to the information just yet. When he found only concern and approval in the man's eyes, Simon nodded. "I do want to ensure Miss Mitchell's safety. But there is another reason I want you to keep an eye on her."

"And what reason is that?" Nat narrowed his gaze, his voice hesitant as though he wasn't sure he liked where Simon was headed.

"I'd like you to tell me if she talks to anyone you don't know. If she does anything strange. If she acts suspicious in any way."

"You think Miss Torey is a scoundrel?" Nat lifted himself to his full height and scowled down at Simon. "If that's what you think, you're mistaken. Miss Torey is a God-fearing girl with a real good heart. I suspect she's been through a rough time of it. But that don't make her bad folk by no means."

Startled by the bodyguard's lack of respect, Simon gave him a stern glance. "I'm not saying she's a scoundrel, Nat. I'm simply saying I have my reasons for you to keep an eye on her. If she's as innocent as you believe, there will be nothing to report back to me, will there? On the other hand, watching her will keep her safe in the event someone—the man you saw tonight, for instance—is out to harm her."

Pausing only for a moment, Nat nodded slowly. "Yes, Sir. I'll keep watch over her. But mostly to protect her. If she does something that looks suspicious, I'll tell you. But I don't think she will."

"Thank you. That's all I ask."

Torey couldn't sleep. Every time she closed her eyes, she imagined sinister sounds and shadows outside her window or right inside her room. She knew Amos couldn't get inside the house without causing a ruckus, but her fear-gripped mind couldn't stop conjuring all the scenarios by which he *might* be capable of coming after her. Terror seized her, despite the presence of the light she'd requested be left on.

When the downstairs clock struck three, she decided to go to the library and get a book to read. She needed something lighthearted and sweet to get her mind off of the wretched reality of Amos and his presence outside earlier.

Something written by Jane Austen, perhaps.

Slipping into dressing gown and house shoes, Torey made her way down the stairs. Her mind continued to swirl, though she desperately wished for peace. If only she could find a way to make Amos agree to leave her alone. What purpose did he have for her? He seemed surprised she was working for the Crawfords, as though he hadn't known that this was their home, and yet he had mentioned Simon. Confusion held her fast, and no matter how hard she tried to figure it out, the truth eluded her.

She went straight to the section of shelves that held the books written by Jane Austen. After selecting *Sense and Sensibility,* one of her favorites, she decided to sit in the chair in front of the warm fire, in which still burned glowing embers. She sighed as she began, her mind slowly switching gears from the fearful images of Amos abducting her to a gentler world, where the girl always got her man in the end.

She read until her eyes grew heavier and heavier. Just as she was dozing off, she sensed movement by the door and jerked awake with a gasp.

"Miss Mitchell?" Simon stood in the doorway fully clothed, though rumpled in appearance. "What are you doing up at this late hour? Or early morning hour, to be more precise."

"I couldn't sleep, so I came down to get a book."

"The coals have practically gone out. You must be freezing in just a nightdress and dressing gown."

Heat suffused her cheeks at his reference to her attire, particularly when she hadn't replaced Georgia's nightdress with one of her own yet, so her ankles stuck out from beneath it. Simon kept his gazed focused away from her bare flesh.

"Yes, Sir. I am cold. I was so enthralled in my book that I didn't notice how cold the room was becoming." She walked toward him, knowing she'd have to pass him to get through the door.

As she reached him, he cleared his throat. "Miss Mitchell, if I may be so bold. . ."

"Yes?" His nearness wreaked havoc on her ability to focus.

"The doctor said you were terrified, and that's why you fainted earlier."

Glancing at the floor, Torey nodded. "I am rather afraid of the dark, I'm embarrassed to say."

Narrowing his gaze, he peered harder, and Torey got the keen sense he was trying to somehow read her expression, tone of voice, anything to discover what he was sure she was hiding from him. "Is there anything you'd like to discuss with me? If you're in trouble or anything. . ."

"Simon, there is nothing I want to discuss with you at this time. But I appreciate your asking. Though I don't know why you would, given my position in your household."

He wrapped his fingers around her forearm. "Because I care about you. If your fear had anything to do with something more than the dark, I'd hope you would feel comfortable enough to come to me and share your concerns."

Torey knew he was anxiously hoping she'd confess something to confirm or deny his suspicions. But she couldn't right now. Besides, she'd promised Mrs. Crawford she wouldn't tell Simon or anyone else about Amos killing that poor man. "I appreciate your concern, Mr. Crawford, but I can't divulge more than you know for now."

His thumb caressed her arm. His gaze took in hers with an intensity that stole Torey's breath away. "Mr. Crawford, please. . ."

He took a step closer. "A moment ago you called me Simon."

"I–I did?"

Nodding, he reached forward and brushed back a strand of loose hair from her cheek. "You have lovely hair."

"Thank you, Mr. Crawford, but really. . ."

"Simon," he said softly, his gaze moving across her face and settling upon her lips.

"What?"

"I wish you'd call me Simon. Mr. Crawford sounds so formal."

"And proper." Torey drew herself up to her full height. Her knees felt like they might not hold her, and her insides quivered wildly, but she knew she had to draw a line. With a determination born of a desire to keep things properly balanced between them, given their stations in life, she pulled her arm from his grasp.

"This isn't proper, Mr. Crawford."

"Maybe I want to court you. Would that be proper?" He didn't try to reach for her arm again; instead he leaned back against the doorframe.

Her heart slammed against her chest wall. "You want to court me?"

He nodded. "What do you think?"

"Oh, Simon. Not now." She leaned wearily against the other side of the doorframe, facing him.

"Of course not now. It's much too early in the morning."

His boyish grin nearly did her in, but she bolstered her

resolve with the memory of Amos's sneering face. "I'm sorry, Mr. Crawford. It just isn't possible."

"I think it is possible. Mother and Katherine are here to keep us properly chaperoned."

Torey glanced around pointedly, then turned her gaze back to him. "Oh, really? Where are our chaperones now?"

His cheeks colored. "Well, they're not here at this second; but believe me, if we were courting, we'd never have chances alone like this. I wouldn't put it past Katherine to sleep outside of your door just to be sure things are kept decent."

Torey giggled but sobered almost immediately. "I am honored by your invitation, and if circumstances in my life were different, nothing could persuade me to refuse your attentions."

Disappointment crossed his features. His face paled. "You care about me too. I can tell."

Releasing a heavy sigh, Torey nodded. "I don't know if it's because, until Robert moved in, we were the only two young people in the house and so it was just natural for us to drift toward each other, or if we would have had a fondness for each other anyway. But the fact remains that it's simply not possible at this time."

Simon shrugged. "All right. I will accept your decision. But I hope you will feel you can confide in me soon."

"I hope so too, Simon. I really hope so. Good night."

With a heavy heart, Torey climbed the stairs to her room. She was aware of Simon's gaze on her as she ascended the steps. And she appreciated that he did her the courtesy of remaining downstairs until she had reached her door.

Simon asking to court her should have made tonight one of the happiest moments of her life. Such a wonderful occurrence after the splendid time they'd had with the children earlier, buying clothes, eating out for lunch. At first the children hadn't seemed to believe they were really getting new clothes, but when the hackney stopped in front of the clothing store, they slowly began to believe, and the excitement built from there.

Climbing into bed, now close to dawn, Torey closed her eyes and relived the encounter with Simon. He sincerely wanted to court her. No dalliance with the hired girl. Courting led to marriage in most cases. Simon was falling in love with her.

Squeezing her eyes tightly, she prayed for all she was worth.

Oh, Lord. Please, if it's Your will, let Simon be patient a bit longer. Perhaps long enough for the police to figure out Amos is the one responsible for that poor man's murder. I can't let our hearts get any more involved in this relationship for now. Not until Amos is no longer a threat to our happiness.

About Amos, Lord—please protect me from him, and show me what to do. . .

eleven

"That's the biggest turkey I've ever seen in my whole life!" Toby said as Katherine washed the enormous bird for the next day's Thanksgiving meal.

"Aw, you ain't never seen a turkey before." Mike scowled, though Torey noticed his eyes were as wide as his siblings'.

Toby sent his brother a fierce glare but didn't retort. Prompted by incessant squabbling and sometimes violent outbursts between the boys, Katherine and Mrs. Crawford had started lessons about how to treat one's fellow man. And if the great spiritual input wasn't enough to keep the children from spatting with each other, Katherine had promised the turkey wishbone to the two who remained the most polite between now and after the bird was carved.

Torey figured Toby had the most at stake. She knew how badly he craved a bicycle. It didn't take a prophet to figure out what he would wish for. She grinned. The miracle would be if the lad could keep his temper in check for another day and a half.

Grabbing two towels, Torey opened the oven door and peeked in on her handiwork. Pride filled her as the heady scent of freshly baked pumpkin pie wafted through the kitchen. The children said "ooh" in unison, licking their lips.

"Let's just hope it tastes as good as it smells," Torey said, setting it on the counter to cool. She pulled out the second one and set it next on the counter as well. "I've never made pumpkin pie before. Or any pie for that matter."

"Maybe we ought to taste one of them to be sure," Tommy said, his face carefully thoughtful.

"The pie's fine. We will wait until tomorrow to sample it." The twinkle in Katherine's eyes belied the gruffness of her tone. "Who wants to help me stuff the turkey?"

"I do!" The twins and Sarah danced around the kitchen, vying for the honor. Mike shook his head. "I ain't sticking my hand inside that bird. Besides, that's women's work."

"Yeah, me neither." Toby came to stand next to his brother, his hands folded across his chest, identical to Mike's stance. "That's women's work."

Tommy followed suit. "Yeah."

A shrug lifted Katherine's shoulders. "Fine. Have it your way. The girls and I will do quite well on our own. In the meantime, you boys may go and bring in some wood to fill the wood bins in all the rooms with fireplaces. That's sufficiently men's work."

"Hey, we don't gotta do no work at all," Mike said, a sneer on his face. "We're paying customers."

"Yeah," Toby replied.

Torey sighed. *Well, at least they've agreeing on something.*

"I'll bring it in," Tommy offered.

The two boys glared at him. "What's the big idea?" Toby demanded.

Tommy lifted his chin stubbornly, fixing his legs hip-width apart, making his stance firm. "I like it here, and I like Miss Katherine. She cooks real good food. If we don't bring in the wood, she'll have to carry it in. And that ain't fair."

Katherine's eyes misted. She cleared her throat. Gone was the gruff exterior. "Thank you, Tommy. You're a real good boy."

"Aw, I'll help." Toby ducked, moving away from Mike as quickly as possible, as though expecting a blow for being a traitor.

Instead, Mike nodded. "Okay. We'll do it. Tommy's right. We ain't never had such good food."

"Well, then," Katherine said, her eyes suspiciously wet.

"First go bundle up. It's snowing. When you get all the wood bins filled, come back to the kitchen, and we'll see what sort of treat we can rummage up as reward."

"Yes, Ma'am!" The boys took off lickety-split.

When they returned, the table was set with a slice of pumpkin pie and a mug of hot chocolate for each child. Torey watched as, one by one, the children, eyes shining, took a first bite. Silently, their gazes darted to one another. Simultaneously, they sipped their chocolate. Slowly, they each took another bite. Then another sip. They continued the routine until they finished their pie. Disappointment slammed into Torey's gut. They could have at least smiled.

"May we be excused?" Mike asked with more politeness than Torey had been aware he possessed.

"Yes. You may go into the library and pick out books to read. Please try to remain quiet as Mrs. Crawford is entertaining in the parlor."

Rather subdued, the children filed out of the kitchen. Torey frowned and expelled a frustrated breath. "Well, for pity's sake. You'd think they'd at least say 'thank you.'"

Waving away the comment, Katherine lifted the last two slices of the pie onto plates and poured two mugs of hot chocolate. She motioned toward the table. Still perplexed and more than a little insulted, Torey sank to a nearby chair and lifted a forkful of the holiday treat to her lips, anticipating the spicy sweetness to come.

"Oh, my." Katherine's exclamation came at the same time bitterness flooded Torey's taste buds. Grabbing a napkin, she expelled the contents of her mouth. She glanced in horror at Katherine, who pushed back the pie plate and sipped her hot chocolate.

"How much sugar did you use?" Katherine asked.

"I–I guess I forgot the sugar." Humiliation lashed at her, burning her cheeks.

Standing, Katherine took their plates and emptied the contents. "Well, it's a good thing we discovered this mistake before we served it tomorrow after dinner."

Torey could have wept. Her first attempt at making a pie. It had looked so wonderful, had even smelled wonderful. A gasp escaped her throat and her hand flew to her cheek.

Katherine turned to her, eyes clouded with concern. "What is it? We can make more pies. There are plenty of jars of pumpkin left in the cellar."

"No! Oh, Katherine, those poor children."

Color drained from the woman's face. "And those little angels never complained. What on earth have they been through that they'll eat what's put before them even if it isn't fit for human consumption?"

So concerned was she over the children, Torey let the "not fit for human consumption" remark slide over her without taking offense. Some things were more important. "Excuse me," she said. "I believe I'll go speak with them."

Katherine nodded.

Torey found the children in the library, the boys each curled up on the sofa. Melissa sat in the wing chair with little Sarah on her lap, reading a book aloud. Even the boys listened quietly. Standing in the doorway, Torey watched them. Suddenly a surge of tenderness raced over her. She knew Robert cared for the children. She admired how hard he worked to make ends meet, but she couldn't help but wonder how many words he actually spoke to them in a day. They needed guidance, love, nurturing. Without those things, children failed to thrive. Torey knew the loneliness of life with an indifferent guardian.

Guilt pricked her at her inward criticism. Robert was up at dawn each day. The boys slept in the same room, so Torey knew his own sleep had to be restless. He worked until five at the bank and went directly to the icehouse, where he loaded and delivered ice first to homes, then to establishments that kept late hours. Torey had heard him coming in after two in the morning more than once. The next day, he started all over again.

The children found their own entertainment, from playing with Abe, to reading, to climbing trees and swinging on the rope swing Simon had fashioned and hung from a sturdy branch in the oak tree outside Torey's window.

Torey shifted and Melissa glanced up. Her eyes questioned. Smiling to put the children at ease, Torey stepped inside.

"What are you reading?" she asked.

"*The Wonderful Wizard of Oz.*" Melissa held up the book for her to see. "Mrs. Crawford said we could."

"Of course. That's a wonderful book." Torey smiled. "May I interrupt you for a minute? I'd like to talk to you about something."

"Yes." Dread clouded Melissa's eyes, and she glanced from one boy to the next.

Torey walked to the fireplace and stood with her back to it, relishing the warmth. She noticed the wood bin filled as high as possible and smiled.

"We didn't do nothin'." Toby scowled.

"I know you didn't do *anything*." She grinned at him. "At least nothing I know about."

"Then how come you want to talk to us?" Tommy asked, a troubled look covering his face. "Did we forget to fill one of the wood bins?"

"I don't think so." She shrugged. "But even so, it's nothing to worry about for now."

"What have we done, Miss Torey?" Melissa's soulful brown eyes spoke a world of responsibility. From their first day living at the Crawfords', it was obvious that she was the little mother figure and took care of the others. She reminded Torey of Wendy from a wonderful play she'd seen in London.

The play *Peter and Wendy* had opened at the Duke of York's Theatre only days after Mother, Amos, and Torey had arrived in the city. A month later, while still abroad, her mother had succumbed to pneumonia. Torey would always cherish the memory of those last days with her mother. They had buried her in London, and Amos and Torey had returned to Chicago alone.

As she looked around at these children's anxious faces, she related to their parentless status once again. Compassion filled her. She smiled. "First of all, everyone calm down. I didn't come in here to fuss at anyone."

All five children relaxed visibly.

"Now, I want to apologize for the pie."

The children exchanged glances; then all eyes focused back on her.

Torey couldn't suppress a giggle, which caused the children to exchange glances again.

"Why are you sorry?" Tommy asked. "We have never had pumpkin pie before."

Melissa nodded. "Uncle Robert says we must always be willing to try new experiences."

Lips twisting into a wry grin at their attempt to smooth things over, Torey shook her head. "All right. Lest I forever taint your view of pumpkin pie, I have to confess something."

Silently the children waited.

"I forgot to put the sugar in the pie." Laughter bubbled up and burst forth from her lips.

"You mean it ain't supposed to taste like that?" Mike's slow grin showed he was catching on.

One by one their expressions changed from caution to amusement; and finally, spurred on by Torey's mirth, the room erupted in childish titters.

"Whew," Toby said. "I wondered why anyone would eat pumpkin pie! I was going to pound William Conn for telling me there wasn't nothin' better to eat. I thought he was just trying to get me to taste something awful."

"Yeah, like the time Mike talked you into tasting that ol' worm."

"Yeah." Toby looked resentfully at his older brother.

In an effort to thwart a fight, Torey addressed Toby. "Lucky for William I made my confession." Torey smiled, and to her surprise the boy gave her a grin in return. She scanned the children's faces. "Promise you'll give it another chance tomorrow? We're making more."

Tommy's eyes twinkled. "If you promise to put sugar in it this time."

Laughter erupted once more. "You have nothing to worry about. I'm sure Katherine won't let me anywhere near the next batch. As a matter of fact, I wouldn't be a bit surprised to go back to the kitchen and discover she's already finished making the crust and is working on the mix."

"Boy, it sure is funny." Mike spoke, and Torey realized by the reflective look on his face that he meant odd-funny and not amusing-funny.

"What do you mean?" she gently prompted.

"That pie. It looked so good. Smelled good too. But when you bit into it. . ." He scrunched his nose.

Torey sensed he wasn't finished with his thought. She nodded encouragement.

He looked straight at her, a frown creasing his brow as though understanding was dawning inside his young mind. "You never know about something just from the outside, do you?"

"No, you never do. Only God knows what's inside."

"Like people." He averted his gaze and stared around Torey into the fire.

"What do you mean?"

"Some people look all spiffy on the outside. And smell all

pretty like flowers. But they're mean on the inside."

Toby snickered. Tommy joined him, and Melissa glanced at Mike, her eyes filled with sympathy.

Mike glared at the twins. "Shut up," he growled.

But the ornery little boys were beyond taking his threat. Toby grabbed Tommy's hand and pretended to kiss it. "Oh, Becky Zimmerman," he said, lowering his voice slightly. "I love you. Be my girl. Oh, Becky, you're so pretty. You smell sooo sweet." The twins clutched their stomachs and howled.

"You better shut up!" Mike shot to his feet and stood over the giggling boys.

Torey was beginning to catch on.

Moving quickly, she stepped between the twelve year old and his tormentors.

"It's all right, Mike."

He gained control, and his eyes stopped flashing anger.

"Want to talk about it?" Torey asked.

"Naw." He scowled.

"All right. If you change your mind, the offer stands."

With a nod, he looked away and shoved his hands into his trouser pockets.

"I'd better get back to the kitchen so I can help Katherine." She wiggled her brows, eliciting more laughter from the children. "If she'll let me anywhere near the baking."

Their chuckles continued.

She walked out of the library. Poor Mike. He was learning the hard way that just because something glittered didn't make it gold. The opposite could be said of these wonderful children. On the outside, they were tough fighters, clinging to everything they had and to each other just to survive. Inside, they were the finest gold. Though she'd come from a privileged home, she knew she was like these children—she'd needed to be given a chance. Despite the menial work, Amos's threats, and the uncertainty of her relationship with Simon,

Torey realized she hadn't been this happy since before her mother's death.

The bell rang as she made her way through the foyer. Torey backtracked and opened the door. A messenger stood on the front step. The lad smiled. "I have a telegram for Victoria Mitchell."

Taken aback, Torey stared at the envelope in his hands.

"Miss?" The messenger's brow creased. "You okay?"

"Oh, of course. I'm sorry. I'm Miss Mitchell." The boy gave her the telegram and waited, smiling.

Torey stared at him until realization dawned. Her cheeks flushed. "I'm sorry. If you'll wait a moment, I'll have to go upstairs to get your tip."

"Thank you, Ma'am."

Tucking the telegram safely in her large apron pocket, Torey ran upstairs, retrieved a coin, and hurried back. With a grin of thanks, the boy tipped his hat and sauntered down the walk.

Dread clenched Torey's stomach. Only one person knew where she was. She slipped her hand into her pocket, then snatched it back as the kitchen door opened and Nat came through.

"Miss Katherine says there's plenty of work still to do for tomorrow and she could use your help."

With a sigh, Torey trailed behind him. The telegram would have to wait until later.

❧

Simon's heart felt light as he closed the wrought-iron gate behind him and made his way up the walk to his home. His once-quiet existence had altered dramatically of late, but he had to admit, the addition of first Torey to their home and then the children had brightened his life. Evenings were no longer long and uneventful. An adventure always lurked around the corner—usually in the form of a prank, disaster, or the simple routine that he was learning was associated with a home where children lived. Feeding, reading to, playing with, and making the children ready for bed consumed a great deal of his time. All the adults pitched in to take care of the children, but in Robert's absence, overseeing the boys' nightly routine fell to Simon. He enjoyed the challenge.

Spicy scents greeted him when he walked inside. From the library, he heard shouts of indignation and scuffling that sounded suspiciously like fighting.

He hurried toward the sounds. On the floor, Mike rolled with Toby. After a second to gauge whether they were play-wrestling or fighting in anger, Simon concluded it was the latter. He strode purposefully to the center of the room and reached down. Grabbing Mike by the arm, he pulled him off his brother. Red-faced and breathing heavily, Mike struggled until he got his bearings and realized who had hold of him.

Simon glanced at Toby. "You okay?" he asked the boy.

With a sneer, Toby wiped a streak of blood away from his nose. "Aw, he can't hurt me."

Melissa came forward quickly, holding firmly to Sarah's hand. "Come on, Toby. Let's go and get you cleaned up."

"I don't need your help," he retorted.

"Go with your sister," Simon said firmly. He looked at Tommy, whose eyes reflected a world of worry. He softened his tone, hoping it would reassure the boy. "You go with them."

After watching them leave, he turned to Mike. "What was that all about?"

"Nothin'," the boy muttered.

"It didn't look like nothing to me." Simon waved him to a chair. "Why don't you sit down for a minute and calm down. Then we can talk about why you would bloody your own brother's nose."

With a ragged breath, Mike took Simon's proffered handkerchief. The boy rested his elbows on his knees, wiping at the sweat dripping from his hairline.

Simon waited while the boy collected himself. After a few silent moments, Mike finally spoke. Like water breaking through a dam, the words spilled forth. "I hate him."

"Toby?"

"My pa." He met Simon's gaze, his eyes flashing in anger.

"What happened tonight to bring this on?"

Tears ran down his cheeks. Simon knew what tears cost a boy as proud as this one. The wrong response could make Mike retreat back into himself. And Simon wanted to help the lad.

"Toby always says I'm like Pa. Look like him, talk like him."

Simon nodded. Toby baited Mike with the comparison, knowing it would cause a negative reaction.

"Tonight he said I ain't good enough to keep a girl interested. Just like Pa lost my ma, I lost Becky."

"I'm afraid I don't understand." Simon leaned forward, matching Mike's position.

"My ma left my pa because she was tired of him drinking all the time and coming home and. . ." He took a deep breath. "And hitting her."

Taken aback by the news, Simon frowned. "But I thought your mother—"

"Was dead?" He gave a snort, and Simon could see the anger building once more. "Uncle Robert tells everyone that to make people feel sorry for us so they won't give us a hard time when we do bad things. Besides, he don't want to tell anyone his brother is a drunk and hits his wife."

Simon nodded. He determined to have a talk with Robert. The children had lost their mother as it was. They didn't need to lose hope that she might return. "You don't know where your mother went?"

"Probably still in New York. When I'm old enough, I'm going back to find her. I know she wants us." Tears flowed.

"How long ago did your mother leave?"

"May. Three days before my birthday. She was going to bake me a lemon cake because it's my favorite."

"Only six months? When did your father bring you to Chicago?"

He shrugged. "A few days later, I guess. But I ain't like him! I'd have made Becky a good beau. I'd never, ever hurt her."

"Becky?"

His face reddened. "A girl at school. But it don't matter."

"She doesn't return your affection, I take it?"

Releasing a heavy sigh, Mike shook his head. "No. She said I wasn't good enough to be her beau."

Simon sympathized with the lad. He was having the same trouble in reverse. Torey refused his attention because she was a servant. "It's difficult to care about someone who doesn't return your affection. But let me assure you, your situation has nothing to do with what happened between your parents."

Mike glanced at him hopefully, and Simon could see the lad wanted him to continue his reassuring discourse. "Son, young ladies will come and go in your life. It seems as though you're more upset because Toby insulted you than you are because of this girl's lack of interest."

"I guess you're right. She's real pretty but sorta mean. Like Miss Torey's pumpkin pie."

"Pumpkin pie?"

"Yeah." Mike grinned through his tears. "It looked good and smelled good but tasted awful! She forgot to put in the sugar."

Simon chuckled. Torey was trying. If nothing else, she'd managed to provide a wonderful illustration that God could use to help Mike understand something about life.

"So you see? Becky is beautiful on the outside but has no sweetness."

"Yep. But what about Pa? Do you think I'm like him?"

A smile tipped Simon's lips. "I think you're a good boy with a lot to be angry about. The Bible doesn't tell us we can't get mad."

The boy's brows shot up. "Really?"

"That's right." Simon fished for the words his own father had given him one day when Simon been angry with a boy. "You can't always control the feelings that creep in. But God has given us all a will."

"A will?"

Simon grinned. "We either will do what's right or we won't."

Mike returned the grin. "I have a will."

"In other words, a choice. In every situation, you get to decide if you let your anger rule you or if you control yourself. People with a good character will control themselves, even when angry."

Nodding slowly, Mike met Simon's gaze. "I don't think I have good character, then." He sighed.

"Son, I'll let you in on a little secret. Actually, it's a mystery really."

"A mystery?"

"Yes. Only people who know God understand this."

Mike leaned forward expectantly, his eyes alight with interest.

"Without God, we are all prone to do whatever we feel like doing. But when you belong to God, He begins to take those impulses—your tendency to fly into your brother when he makes you mad, for instance—and He convicts you just as you're about to let go with your fists. He might say something like, 'Don't do it! It's not right.' So the fight is stopped before it's begun. Eventually, after you learn to listen to that little voice in your heart, you realize one day that your brother doesn't set you off nearly as much as he used to."

"You really think I can stop wanting to pound Toby when

he cracks off to me?"

"I know it."

"Do you think God would want me?"

Simon's heart leaped. His nerves were taut. He felt like the worst kind of hypocrite, considering his own feelings about God since Father's death; but somehow he knew that he couldn't let this opportunity to share the gospel with this boy pass by. "I know He does. He sent His Son, Jesus, to die on the cross for one reason—so that all men would be able to live with Him in heaven one day."

"How do I. . .?"

"Do you believe that Jesus is God's Son?"

He nodded.

"Do you believe what I just told you, about God sending Jesus to die on the cross? And that He rose from the dead three days later?"

Again, Mike nodded.

"Then tell Him so. Ask Him to forgive your sins and invite Him to be your Lord. If you tell Him you'd like to belong to Him, He'll come and live on the inside of you, and, Mike, you'll be a new person."

He frowned. "I don't understand. I won't be Mike anymore?"

"Let's put it this way. You'll begin to think differently and act differently. When God lives in you, sin can't stay. Now that doesn't mean you won't ever sin, because we all do. But you'll repent immediately, and God will wash that sin away. Would you like to ask God to make you His?"

Mike nodded, tears flooding his eyes.

Simon took his hand, and he knew heaven rejoiced.

twelve

What sort of game was Amos playing? Torey frowned and reread the telegram. It made no more sense today than it had a week ago when she'd received it:

DOES SIMON CRAWFORD ENJOY THE THEATRE? STOP ASK HIM, AND I'LL BE WAITING FOR YOU TO COME HOME STOP

Why would Amos care? Besides, if he thought anything would induce her to go back home, he was sorely mistaken.

With a sigh, she slipped the telegram back under her pillow. Still reading the question in her mind, she shrugged into her coat and wrapped her scarf around her neck. She could hear the children scuffling around in the hallway. No doubt trying to gather the courage to knock on her door and hurry her along.

She smiled. Simon had borrowed a wagon, and today they were going to the Clark Street Bridge to buy a Christmas tree. The Chicago River famously hosted the Christmas ship. Every year, the captain brought trees from Michigan and sold them right off the deck. It was quite the custom, and many of Torey's friends and neighbors considered the ship's docking to be the beginning of the Christmas season.

Since Thanksgiving Day, the excitement had been building in the children. Simon had promised to take them to pick out a tree today. And of course, he'd insisted Torey ride along.

Torey checked her reflection in the vanity mirror. Satisfied that her hair was in place, she stepped into the hallway, pulling her gloves from her pockets.

"Are you finally ready?" Toby asked, his eyes shining with anticipation. He looked like a Roman candle about to go off.

"I sure am." Torey grinned at the look of relief crossing his features. "What about Mr. Crawford?"

"Yep. He's already in the wagon."

"Then let's not keep him waiting any longer." She ruffled his shock-white hair. "Put on your hat."

He complied, and the boys nearly flew down the stairs, each trying to move ahead of the other two.

"Careful!" Torey shouted. She shook her head, her lips twitching. "Those boys. They have one speed—fast."

Melissa grinned. "That's the truth."

Sarah reached up and took Torey's hand. " 'Cept at chore time," she said with a grin.

The three of them giggled all the way down the steps.

Though fresh snow had fallen the night before, the sun shone brilliantly this morning. Torey took a deep breath of the crisp, clean air.

"It's about time," Simon said good-naturedly as he hopped down from the driver's seat. "Children in the back of the wagon." He bowed to Torey. "Your chariot awaits you, Milady."

Giggles from the children brought a rush of warmth to Torey's cheeks. She kept her gaze away from Simon's as she accepted his help into the seat.

He took his place beside her, grabbed the reins, and winked at her as he turned to the children. "I want to hear everyone singing, 'Jingle bells, jingle bells, jingle all the waaay.' " The children joined in, making a merry noise.

They turned many, many heads during the five-mile trip between the house and Clark Street, but Torey didn't care. She was thrilled that the children were enjoying themselves. This had to be the worst time of year for children whose parents were dead and whose uncle worked incessantly to make ends meet.

She had tucked money aside to buy gifts. Her only sorrow was that she couldn't buy Toby the bicycle he so desperately wanted. If only Amos hadn't turned out to be such a crook and hadn't gambled away her inheritance. Dread hit her stomach at his unwelcome intrusion into her otherwise perfect morning. But at the reminder of him, the words on the telegram scrolled across her mind.

Simon was just singing the last bar of "Silent Night, Holy Night." The children were peaceful and quietly watched the snowy road roll by. Torey touched Simon's arm.

He looked at her, and Torey returned his gaze, transfixed by the longing in his eyes. "Yes?" he said, just above a whisper.

"I—I need to ask you something."

"What is it?"

Gathering a steadying breath, she forged ahead. "D—do you like the theatre?"

His face clouded. "Why do you ask?"

"I don't know. I just wondered."

"You just wondered?" The cynicism in his tone took her aback.

"Yes." Torey looked down at her lap. "Please, forget I asked. I didn't mean to upset you."

She felt his hand cup her face and she turned. He studied her, brow furrowed. "Are you telling me you don't know how my father died?"

Torey's pulse began to race. She shook her head.

He released her and looked toward the road. Releasing a sigh, he began, "My father and I went to see a Verdi opera at the auditorium one night. Father was feeling a bit poorly by the time it was over, so I told him to wait in the booth while I pushed through the crowd and ordered the hackney to take us home. Paul, the driver, is usually on time, but that night he was delayed, so I waited a few extra minutes for him to show up."

Panic hit Torey's stomach. Fear. Torment. She wanted to cover her ears and scream at the top of her lungs so she didn't have to hear the rest of the all-too-familiar story. By the look of horror on Simon's face, Torey knew he was reliving the incident.

She saw it too—every second of that terrible night. Tears filled her eyes. *Amos knows!* That's why he thought she'd hitched herself to the Crawfords—to somehow extort money from their tragedy. Oh, what a wretched, evil man her step-father was!

"I–I found him on the floor, stabbed through the chest." A shudder began deep within Simon as he revealed the last of his tale. "If only I had gotten there sooner. I might have scared the thief away. Or maybe I could have saved my father."

"There was nothing you could do, Simon. He was dead instantly."

He turned to her sharply, and Torey realized her mistake. In her effort to comfort him, she'd almost given herself away.

"What do you mean?" he demanded. "How could you possibly know if he died instantly or not?"

"Y–you said you found him with a knife in his chest. I just assumed. I'm sorry."

"Wookie!" The sound of Sarah's excited voice broke the tension for the moment, and Torey turned her attention forward, taking little pleasure in the beautiful ship docked at the bridge and filled with evergreens waiting to become Christmas trees.

Simon didn't look at her as he helped her from the wagon. Torey felt like weeping. She blinked back the tears that stung her eyes and tried to swallow around the lump in her throat. The children ran, boarding the ship ahead of Simon and Torey.

"Simon, I—"

"We can discuss it later, Miss Mitchell. Let's not put a damper on the children's day."

Torey nodded. "You're right, of course."

Silently, they walked the gangplank and went their separate ways once they stepped on deck. For Torey, the day had lost its magic. Disappointment and despair made poor companions as she walked between the rows of evergreens. The beauty of the snow-tipped branches failed to take her breath away as it would have even an hour ago.

Dear Lord, what will I do? How could I have fallen in love with the son of the man Amos killed? It's difficult not to question Your ways in this. My heart wants to ask how You could let this happen. But the part of me that is learning to trust You knows that You are sovereign and have Your reasons. Help me, Lord. And please help Simon when he learns the truth.

Tears accompanied the silent plea. As quickly as she wiped them away, they were replaced, and she couldn't stop the onslaught.

Sudden pain shot through her arm, and she felt a hand over her mouth. "Don't scream, or I'll slit your throat. Do you understand?" Fear gripped her and held her fast as she recognized the voice and got a whiff of the brandy-scented breath.

Torey nodded, feeling the cold steel pressed again the tender skin of her neck.

Amos uncovered her mouth but held her fast. "Let's go to the back of the ship behind those trees." He pressed her arm, and she accompanied him with no protest or struggle, knowing he couldn't get her off the ship without Simon spotting them. A disturbing thought came to her. In light of their earlier conversation, would Simon bother to attempt to stop her if Amos tried to kidnap her? How far did his suspicions go?

When they reached their destination, Amos jerked her around roughly. His eyes glittered hard. "There's no one to save you this time."

"Wh—what do you want?"

"Did you get my message?"

Loathe to grant him mercenary pleasure, Torey was sorely tempted to lie. She stared back unblinking. He let out a short laugh. "I see you received it. And did you ask young Mr. Crawford how he enjoys the theatre?"

She wanted to slap the sneer from his face. Why had she never noticed what an unattractive man he was? At one time, she'd been proud when her friends called Amos her father. When they said he and her mother made a handsome couple. Now, the sight of him sickened her.

Again, he'd read her correctly. "And so you know the truth about the man at the theatre that night."

"Why did you do it?" She barely recognized the sound of her voice.

"As you are aware by now, your mother's money is gone. Including your inheritance."

He didn't bother to pretend remorse, and Torey didn't expect any such thing. She listened, trying to make sense of what would cause someone to commit the act she'd witnessed of Amos. He went on. "I convinced several wealthy men in town to back me in a business venture. It was supposed to be a sure thing. But before I could make good, I discovered my partner betrayed me. He took the money and left—out of the country by now, I am sure."

Torey couldn't help enjoying the irony that the crook had been robbed. Her pleasure was short-lived, however, when she realized that the situation had led to Amos's actions that night.

"No doubt you are aware that Mr. Crawford was president of the Savings and Loan."

She nodded.

"I went to him that day, humbled myself before him." His eyes flashed his anger. "He refused to loan me the money to pay my debts."

"So you decided to kill him?" Torey's voice rose in incredulity.

"No, I overheard Simon telling a fellow worker that he and his father would be attending the opera that evening. I thought if Mr. Crawford saw me in the same social circle as himself, he might understand that I'm not some two-bit gambler."

"A two-bit gambler? You borrowed money to play cards?"

"Of course not. Horses."

"Y—your business venture was a *horse?*" Torey couldn't contain her revulsion at the thought.

His eyes narrowed dangerously. "I'll not have you standing in judgment of me."

Torey winced as his fingers bit cruelly into her arm. "I'm not standing in judgment, Amos."

He relaxed his grip. She released a slow breath.

"That horse was a sure thing. It had never lost a race. And it won that day. Do you know how rich I would have been if that little weasel hadn't stolen from me? I was desperate. I went to Mr. Crawford a broken man. And what did he do? He looked at me as though I were no better than a two-bit gambler in a card game."

Torey looked past him, and her breath caught. Mike stood at the end of the row of trees, a scowl on his face. She didn't know how much he'd heard, but he looked as though he might come to her rescue. Shaking her head as hard as she dared, she attempted to discourage him. To her relief, he slowly backed away.

"And so that brings us to you, my dear."

Jerking her attention back to Amos, Torey nodded as though she'd heard everything. "I told you I'm happy with the Crawfords."

"Surely you realize it isn't possible for you to stay there now."

"I—I just don't know. I suppose you're right." Though she hated to admit it, Amos had a point. How on earth was she going to look Mrs. Crawford or Simon in the eye after what she'd discovered today?

"Here's what you're going to do," Amos said. "As much as I'd like to force you home right now, I don't want anyone to think you've been kidnapped and come looking for you. So, you'll go to the Crawford home and quit. Explain that you've decided to go home."

"I don't think Mrs. Crawford will believe that."

"Make her believe it!" The snarl on his face conveyed utter evil.

Torey drew back. "Yes, Amos."

"And don't think you can run away again. I will be following you, as I did today." He sneered. "When you walk out the door, I'll be waiting for you."

Not doubting his words one bit, Torey shuddered. Defeat filtered through her.

"Why do you want me home, Amos? What are these plans you have for me?"

"I suppose I can tell you. Mr. Shepherd wants you, and he's willing to pay off my debts when I deliver you to him."

A gasp escaped Torey's lips. "You would sell me?" Had the man no scruples left? He'd squandered her inheritance, had killed a man, and now this?

"I wish there were another way. But I'm afraid I have no choice, my dear." Amos leered. "But don't worry. Mr. Shepherd has assured me he will treat you very well—and he is even willing to marry you. As long as you give him no trouble."

"I won't do it, Amos! I won't marry a man I don't love just to pay off your debts."

In a flash, his hand shot out, landing hard across her cheek.

"You will do as you're told."

She stood her ground. "I won't. I'm in love with Simon." She glared at Amos. "I realize that I will never have him now. But I won't give myself to another man as long as I live."

His eyes glittered, and she thought he might slap her again. Instead, he leaned forward until she could feel his breath hot on her face. "It would be terrible if the same fate befell young Mr. Crawford as did his father."

Cold fear slipped down Torey's spine. "Are you saying. . . ?"

"Make no mistake. I have nothing to lose. If you don't go willingly to Mr. Shepherd, I'm a dead man anyway. Killing another man won't make a difference as far as I'm concerned. It's your choice."

Tears filled her eyes. "I will do as you ask."

"Good girl. Now what are you going to say to the old lady?"

Resentment burned in Torey at Amos's disrespectful manner toward Mrs. Crawford. "I'll tell her I want to go home."

"Good. Don't dawdle. Do it immediately. I'll be waiting for you just after sundown."

"Yes, Amos."

"And, Torey? If you tell anyone that I killed Mr. Crawford, I will most certainly stress your involvement in the murder. You will not get away punishment free."

"I know, Amos." If he only knew how little she cared about that right now. All she cared about was keeping Simon safe.

❧

Shaking in anger, Simon hurried across the deck before Torey emerged from the row of trees. He'd been concerned for her! He'd actually been concerned when Mike had told him Torey was talking to a man and it looked like she was upset about something. After the incident a couple of weeks earlier where Nat had seen her talking to a man and she'd fainted in fear, he'd been ready to do whatever he had to do in order to save her.

All these weeks, he'd come to believe Torey cared about him. She'd played them for fools. The first night, she'd gained Mother's sympathy by appearing distraught and homeless. She'd wormed her way into his heart so that he'd actually been toying with the idea of proposing marriage. True, they hadn't formally courted, but their relationship had developed under unusual conditions, considering they lived in the same house. She'd played that one well.

But what did she want? Why had she come in the first place? Was their plan that she infiltrate the home and steal documents from Father's study? He'd like to confront her. To force her to tell him the truth. But he wouldn't. No, he'd let the police deal with her and the man. The murderer. Rage burned within his chest.

He wished he'd have overheard more, but he only reached the last row of trees in time to hear the man tell her he'd meet her at sundown. That was hours away. He had time to take the children home and call the police while everyone decorated the tree.

⋙

Amos watched Torey ride away with Simon Crawford and the wagon full of children. From somewhere deep in the recesses of his memory, an unwelcome thought shot to the forefront. He remembered his wife's dying request: "Promise me you'll always take care of her."

He'd lifted her weak, clammy hand to his lips and smiled through tears. "I promise, my love." He had trembled, fighting tears as he watched the life slip from the woman he loved.

Her once lovely, full lips had curved into a smile of peace at his reassurance that Torey would be cared for.

Guilt nipped at him as he walked down the gangplank and into the crowd. But with no money to hire a hackney, and his horses sold long ago, he had a five-mile walk to the Crawfords'. Five miles to give his conscience time to abate. Five miles. Worth every step in order to make sure Torey didn't run away again. He'd watch the house all day if he had to. Just in case her love for Simon Crawford wasn't as strong as she'd indicated, and she decided his life wasn't worth the effort of marrying John Shepherd, after all.

A satisfied smile curved his lips. By tomorrow, all his troubles would be over.

thirteen

A single tear slipped down Torey's cheek. Then another and another until her vision blurred, and she was forced to glance up from the letter she was attempting to compose. She knew she could never face Mrs. Crawford without confessing the entire situation and taking a chance Simon might be killed, so she had opted to write a letter instead of risking a face-to-face good-bye.

Amos's contacts were extensive. Even if he were sitting in jail, he might be able to get to Simon. And as much as she'd like to see her stepfather pay for his heinous crime, Simon's life meant too much for her to take the chance.

She signed the letter. While she waited for the ink to dry, she walked to the wardrobe. Fingering the cloth of the gowns, she thought back to how excited she'd been to buy the two serviceable gowns and one more church dress to accompany the one she'd bought the day Simon had introduced her to corned beef and cabbage. With a sigh, she closed the wardrobe again without bothering to remove anything. These gowns wouldn't be suitable in her new life. Mr. Shepherd would buy her silks and satins. He'd never allow her to wear coarser materials or anything less than the best. After all, a man's reputation must be preserved.

The dresses could easily be made over for Melissa. The girl would be thrilled to have them. Torey smiled a little at the thought and sat to write another note, requesting that Mrs. Crawford present the gifts to the girl.

A knock at the door interrupted her, and she jumped. No

one must know of her plans. She gathered a deep breath and tried to sound as normal as possible. "Who is it?"

"Mike. We're about to decorate the Christmas tree."

The last thing Torey wanted to do was try to pretend to be festive, but she knew she'd have some explaining to do if she didn't join the rest of the household for the occasion. Sundown was still a couple of hours away. A sigh lifted and lowered her chest. She had no choice.

"Please tell Mrs. Crawford I'll be down in a minute."

"Okay. Uh, we can't start until you come."

A smile tipped her lips. According to the children, they'd never had much of a Christmas tree before. All day, the atmosphere had buzzed with their excitement. Torey could imagine how excruciating the wait must be. Still, there were other matters to attend to. "I'll hurry. I promise."

She heard the sound of his boots shuffling along the hallway and breathed a sigh of relief that he'd taken the hint and wasn't going to wait for her.

Slipping the note she written for Simon into her apron pocket, Torey blinked away quick tears. This home represented the first real happiness she'd known since her mother's death. The first real security.

As slowly as she could, she walked down the hallway to the steps, savoring every inch of the three-foot-wide space, memorizing every crack in the wood. As she descended the stairs, she drank in the scents of lavender and spice. No house had ever smelled as lovely as this one. Wonderful aromas always wafted from the kitchen. Mrs. Crawford used a touch of lavender-scented perfume, and the smell lingered throughout the house.

High-pitched voices drifted from the front room where Nat and Simon had set up the Christmas tree. Torey took a deep breath and detoured to the right, toward the study where she planned to slip the letter onto Simon's desk. She headed down the main hall, then stopped short of rounding the corner. She heard Simon's voice speaking over the newly installed telephone.

"Yes, Captain. That's what I'm telling you. I have discovered the whereabouts of my father's killer."

Stifling a gasp, Torey shrank back against the wall. She knew she shouldn't eavesdrop, but nothing could have driven her from that spot.

"His accomplice has been living under my roof for months, unbeknownst to me." The bitterness in his voice nearly took Torey's breath away. He despised her. "Yes. I heard them discussing the matter. The killer seemed to think himself very clever. He'll be meeting the girl at sundown, and they'll be leaving together. I do not know where they are going, so I would advise you to take advantage of the opportunity to apprehend them. No. I can't identify the man. I didn't see him. I only overheard them."

Torey's heart crashed. Simon had heard enough of their conversation to become aware that Amos had killed his father but not enough to realize she'd only witnessed the murder. He believed her to be an accomplice. She fingered the envelope in her pocket. What was the use of trying to explain things now? He'd never believe her.

"I'm not sure of the girl's motives. She's had access to all of Father's documents. I'm sure a search of her person will reveal something."

The disdain in his tone was unbearable. Slowly, Torey backed away and fled down the hall. She was just about to ascend the steps when she heard Mrs. Crawford's voice from the doorway of the living room.

"Torey? The children are waiting for you. We're about to decorate the tree."

Desperately attempting to compose herself, Torey molded her lips into a smile and turned to face the woman. "Yes,

Ma'am." She searched for an excuse, any excuse to relieve herself of the obligation. But one look at the determination on Mrs. Crawford's face convinced her of the futility of immediate escape.

With clenched fists, she entered the living room, praying for the strength to keep the tears at bay for just a little longer.

❧

Simon placed the telephone receiver on the box and walked into Father's study, a weary sigh escaping him. Sorrow upon sorrow. First Father's death, and now the woman he loved turned out to be involved in the murder.

He sat back in the leather chair, stroking his moustache as he contemplated how he could have been played for such a fool.

"Simon?"

He glanced up at the sound of his mother's voice in the doorway.

"What is it, Mother?"

"You're missing all the fun. We thought you might enjoy putting on the star."

"That's Father's job," he said dully, not sure why he even made such a ridiculous statement.

Mother walked to the desk and stared at him from the other side. "I told the children that it used to be his job, and they insisted the honor must now fall to you."

"I'm sorry, Mother. I'm not in the mood."

In a flash, she slapped the desk hard with the palm of her hand. "I want to know what is going on between you and Torey. Did you have a lovers' spat?"

"Lovers'? Don't be absurd. There's nothing between myself and the maid."

A scowl darkened her face. "Oh, so she's the maid now, is she?"

"She always has been." Simon tried hard to remain nonchalant. Mother would have to be informed, but for now, he wanted to give her the pleasure of her holiday decorating.

"Perhaps, but it's obvious you've fallen in love with her. I know something's happened between you two, because she is in the living room right now pretending to have a good time, when all the while, she's been fighting back tears for the better part of an hour."

Simon jerked his chin and captured Mother's gaze. "What do you mean?"

"As if you didn't know."

Releasing a sigh, Simon decided to go ahead and tell her. She was going to find out in an hour anyway. "Mother, you need to know something. . ." This was going to break her heart. "Sit down, please."

Her gaze flickered over his face and she nodded. When she was seated, Simon leaned forward and reached for her hands. With a frown, she slipped her plump hands in his. "What is it, Son?"

"There's no easy way to tell you this, but Torey will be leaving us tonight."

Mother jerked her hands from his. "What? What did you do to her?"

"I didn't do anything, and I'll explain as soon as you calm down."

She folded her hands in her lap and nodded. "Explain, then."

Simon recounted the overheard conversation, carefully watching Mother's expression. Her lips pressed into a grim line, and her eyes flashed anger.

"And so she will be leaving in a few moments," Simon concluded.

She shot to her feet. "No, my boy, she will not."

"Mother, I know you love the girl, but don't you see? She's not who she claimed to be. She's involved with Father's death and has come to further our grief by finishing whatever it was they left undone."

"Oh, Simon. I've known of Torey's involvement from the night the Lord sent her to us."

"What?" Disbelief shot through him. "You knew she helped kill Father and you just stood by and watched while I fell in love?" A sense of betrayal almost as strong as the one he felt over Torey's actions slithered through him. He felt ill.

"Now, it's your turn to calm down. I vow we are cut from the same cloth. As to Torey's supposed involvement, the only thing that girl is guilty of is being in the wrong place at the wrong time and witnessing a murder. She told me that much. And she told me that she ran away for fear her stepfather would implicate her in the crime although she was innocent."

"She knew, yet she never told me?"

"She didn't know who the man was. There are no photographs or paintings of your father on the walls. Only in my locket."

"All right, let's assume she didn't know. You did. Why didn't you tell me any of this sooner? This man could have been locked away months ago."

"Because, Son, some things are more important than revenge."

"What could be more important than Father's killer brought to justice?"

"The condition of your heart," she said quietly.

A scowl twisted Simon's face. "What has one to do with another?"

"If I had gone to the police when Torey arrived, you would have had your revenge. And you never would have forgiven the man who killed your father."

"I can't forgive him. It's too much for anyone to ask."

"And yet our Lord forgave His murderers even while He hung in agony on the cross. Son, I am convinced of one thing. My husband forgave his killer before he took his last breath. How can we do less?"

Tears clogged Simon's throat at the memory of his father. The pleading in his eyes as the life slipped from him. *"Giiieee. . ."* Father wanted him to get the man who killed him. He'd said so. Hadn't he?

Giiieee. . .

The memory hit Simon in the gut. "Father wasn't saying 'get him,' was he?"

His mother shook her head. "He was a righteous man. A good man. He never would have asked his son to exact revenge on his behalf. It wasn't in his character."

Giiieee. . .

Simon drew in a sharp breath as he realized what Father had been trying to say. *Forgive.* Father had been asking him to forgive the man who had murdered him. Tears formed in Simon's eyes. He'd always wanted to be like his father. Had always striven to be kind to his fellow man, generous to those less fortunate, loving to his mother. All those things he'd witnessed every day of his life. But Simon realized something as the tears formed a stream running down his face. His father had striven to be like one man: Jesus. That's what had made him so special.

"You're right, Mother." Simon took his handkerchief from his pocket. "Father wouldn't have asked for revenge."

Mother's breath released in a slow stream, as though she'd been holding it for a long, long time. "He died as he lived— pure in heart."

Simon gave a defeated shrug. "So where does that leave us now? I've found the killer, and the police are probably waiting right now to arrest him."

"Police?" Mother's eyes narrowed. "What do you mean, the police? Simon, what did you do?"

"I'm sorry, Mother. I called the station house an hour or so ago."

"Oh, Simon," she groaned. "I wish you had spoken with me first. Now Torey might be arrested as well. Especially if that despicable stepfather of hers makes good on his threat to implicate her. We need to warn her before she goes to meet him."

Simon didn't move. He realized the ramifications of warning Torey. If she didn't meet her stepfather, he wouldn't show himself, and would most certainly get away. He loved her, but was his love stronger than his desire to see justice for his father?

In an instant, he made his decision.

fourteen

It wasn't quite sundown, but Torey knew if she was going to have the opportunity to get away, she'd better take it now while neither Simon nor Mrs. Crawford was present.

She excused herself from the festivities, wishing for all she was worth that things were different—that she could stay and continue watching the children's expressions of awe as they stared at the lovely tree, now decorated with strands of beads draped over its branches and glass ornaments molded in the shape of trumpets, birds, bells, and angels.

A war raged inside of her—the same battle she'd been fighting since overhearing Simon speaking with the police. If she went to meet Amos, the police would catch her. Vivid images of herself hanging from the gallows shot through her mind. Placing her hand to her neck, she shuddered.

If she didn't go, Amos would get away and then make good on his threat to harm Simon.

Two choices loomed before her, but she could only consider one of them. She couldn't allow Simon to be killed. Or anyone else. There was no time to go upstairs for her coat. She could bear the cold for a short while. It was little discomfort compared to how cold and empty the rest of her life would be without Simon Crawford.

Forcing herself not to cry, she slipped through the foyer and into the kitchen. She clenched her fists to stop her hands from trembling. Her heart pounded. *Give me courage, Lord.* Drawing a deep breath, she opened the back door.

❧

As the sun descended in the pewter sky, Amos knew he was

finally getting everything he'd been dreaming of. Soon his debts would be paid, and he would be free to move on. Somewhere people didn't know of this disastrous few months. Hidden behind the gazebo, he watched the door open and held his breath. A smile twisted his lips as he spotted Torey. Even in common clothes, she was beautiful. So much like her mother.

He pushed the thought aside. Promises notwithstanding, he had no choice but to take the girl to Mr. Shepherd.

Torey stepped onto the porch, her movements cautious. Her gaze darted about. No doubt she was looking for him. Like a fool, he'd forgotten to tell her where they would meet. He stepped away from the gazebo. The movement caught her eye. She nodded and moved in his direction.

❧

Simon scanned the room and frowned as the children vied for his attention. "Wookie, Mr. Crawford!" Sarah tugged at his suit coat and pointed at the tree. "Isn't it pwetty?"

He smiled. "Yes, Sweetheart, it is. Lovely."

"Are you going to put the star on top now?"

Simon looked back at five expectant little faces. Their expressions told him how desperately they wanted to see the finished product. But there were more important tasks to attend to at the moment. "I'll put it on in a little while, all right? I have to find Miss Torey right now. Do any of you know where she went?"

One by one, they shook their heads.

He glanced outside. The clouds had hampered a marked sunset, but the sky was growing darker. His throat tightened, and he dashed from the living room and headed through the foyer. He flung open the front door. There was no sign of Torey, but three men crept along the sides of the house. They signaled to him to get back inside. "Wait," he said, his voice hoarse. "I've made a mistake."

The chief scowled and motioned harder for him to return to the house.

Panic rose at the thought of Torey being caught in gunfire. He sped through the foyer and kitchen and flung open the door. His throat went dry at the sight of Torey on the ground, her hands behind her back. A massive police officer yanked her to her feet.

Simon saw red. "Get your hands off of her! She hasn't done anything." He looked at the man next to her. "Tell them!"

Amos sneered. "I don't know what she told you, but my stepdaughter tends to be a bit eccentric. You can't trust a word she says."

The man's face struck a chord of memory in Simon's mind. Now he realized why Torey had seemed so familiar when she'd first arrived. The night his father had died, Simon had been on his way up the steps when she'd stumbled into him. He had retrieved her slipper for her. He remembered the raw fear in her eyes, the expression of horror on her drained, white face. Amos had stepped forward and called her eccentric that evening too. But Simon recalled thinking what a pity the girl had such a bully for a father.

"Officer, I recall seeing this man on the steps of the auditorium the night my father died. And I overheard his confession this morning at the Christmas ship. But the girl has nothing to do with it. I insist that you let her go."

The chief stepped forward, a scowl firmly etched into his face. "Earlier you insisted we arrest them both."

"Hey! What are you doin' with Miss Torey?"

Mike, Toby, Tommy, Sarah, and Melissa marched single file down the steps and right up to the chief. "You in charge here?" Toby asked, tilting his head to look the man in the eye.

"Yeah, I guess I am. What do you know about all this?"

"Nothin'!" Toby sneered. "But I know somethin'."

A slight twitch of moustache betrayed the chief's amusement.

"Oh? And what's that?"

"You ain't takin' Miss Torey nowhere. She's about as nice as they come. For a girl. And I'll fight your whole police army if I have to."

"Oh, Toby." Torey's eyes filled with tears. "Honey, I have to do what the policemen say I must. Please show respect."

The boy's expression slowly relaxed, his stormy eyes calmed. "Well, he ain't takin' you nowhere," he mumbled, kicking at the snowy ground.

Mother and Katherine appeared at the door. "What's going on here?"

Simon inwardly groaned, and from the look of irritation on the chief's face, the man felt much the same way.

"This is Torey's stepfather," Simon explained. "He was trying to force her to leave."

"Don't wet them take Miss Torey away," Sarah said, tugging at Mother's apron. "We wuv her."

"We'll try our best, Sweetheart. Now, go on up to the house."

When the little girl had gone, Mother turned her attention to Amos. Her eyes glittered hard as she stared at the man who had murdered the love of her life. Her face clouded, and tears misted her eyes. "I could easily hate you for what you've done," she said. "You have no idea of the treasure you removed from this earth. But I won't allow my soul to be smudged with the sin of unforgiveness."

"Religion!" Amos spat upon the ground. "Your husband tried to spout religion to me too. But I showed him that he couldn't make a fool of me!"

"I'd say that pretty much constitutes a confession, wouldn't you, Chief?" Simon was hard-pressed to keep from tearing into the man. But from deep inside, he heard his father's words. *Love the world, Simon. To be like Jesus, we must love those who wrong us, just as we do those who praise us.*

"That's good enough for me," the chief said with a nod.

"Now as to the girl. . ."

Mother stepped forward quickly. "You don't honestly plan to take Torey away? The girl's done nothing wrong."

The chief looked at the officer who still had a grip on Torey's arm. "Did you search her?"

The officer nodded and held out a document. A lump formed in Simon's throat. He swallowed hard. Had he been mistaken? Was Torey an accomplice after all?

"Please." Torey's small voice broke through. "That's nothing of importance. Give it back."

Simon turned to her, and concern clutched him. Her face was drained of color, and she looked as though she might succumb to a dead faint at any second.

The chief ignored her and continued to read. When he finished, he handed the document to Simon. "I think you'll want to see this."

"No," Torey said weakly.

Swallowing hard, he accepted the proffered document. If she was playing him and his mother for fools, he wanted to know about it!

He looked down and took in a sharp breath.

Dear Simon,

My heart aches at the thought of what I must tell you. But before you read further, please believe me when I tell you, I've fallen in love with you.

Simon looked up from the letter. Torey's lips trembled, and she refused to meet his gaze. He turned his attention back to the letter.

When I came to your home, I was broken and sick, and you and your mother took me in. What you didn't know was that I was running away because I saw my stepfather commit a murder. *I was scared and couldn't think quickly enough to save the man, who I now know was your father. Oh, Simon, I was positively ill when I discovered the man's identity. Now, I'm being forced to go away, as my stepfather has discovered my whereabouts.*

Please forgive me for not revealing his identity and thus seeing him brought to justice. But I fear for your safety and that of your mother. The man my mother once loved has proven to be capable of almost anything.

By the time you read this, I will be gone. Please thank your mother for her kindness to me. I found Jesus in this home, and I will never forget you.

Yours forever,
Victoria Mitchell

Simon glanced up again, this time more than sure Torey had no involvement in his father's death. She was as much an innocent victim in all of this as he was. And she loved him. The thought hit him hard. After all the weeks of keeping him at bay, she'd finally admitted it. He looked at her again. Stepping close, he took her hands in his.

She lifted her head to look at him, and her eyes were filled with uncertainty. Simon didn't blame her. Theirs was a difficult situation. But not something they couldn't work through.

Simon had no time to convey that sentiment to Torey as the burly chief took hold of Amos's arm and jerked him forward. "All right, Bub," he said. "Let's go."

"What about the girl, Chief?" another officer asked.

"Bring her down to the station so we can get a statement from her." He eyed Simon. "We'll want a signed statement from you too, since you overheard his confession. That oughta be enough to put him away."

Simon slipped his arm about Torey's shoulders and pulled her close. He focused on the chief. "What about Miss Mitchell?"

He shrugged. "She's free to leave as soon as we get her statement."

Torey's face showed astonishment. "Y—you mean I'm not going to jail?"

"What for? You didn't murder the man."

From the steps, the children cheered.

Obviously not convinced, Torey frowned. "B—but how do you know I'm innocent?"

"I've been a policeman for a lot of years, Miss. There's no evidence you did anything wrong. Now we have you as an eyewitness against this man."

"Wait!"

Dread hit Simon hard at the sound of Amos's voice. He feared he knew what the man was about to do.

"What do you want?" the officer to Amos's right asked gruffly.

"That girl is every bit as guilty as I am."

"Is that so?" the chief asked, a sneer to match Amos's twisting his features.

Amos's eyes glittered hard. "Why else would she have ended up as a maid at the Crawfords' home?" A short laugh emitted from his lips. "She's never done a day's work in her life. Isn't it obvious she just wanted to get to young Crawford here?"

The chief glanced at Simon and raised his brow. "What do you think?"

An ironic little smile curved Simon's lips, and he was suddenly glad for the months of uncertainty about Torey. "Well, Chief," he drawled, "if Miss Mitchell had set her cap for me, it was the best-kept secret in the Crawford household."

The children laughed uproariously. "She won't even look at him!" Mike hollered. "Thinks it ain't proper 'cause she's just the maid." Single file, they ventured off the porch and joined the adults.

A grin stretched the chief's mouth, and he looked at Torey. She blushed furiously. "I have a feeling all that's about to change," he said.

"It's about time," Mother said, smiling fondly at Torey.

In an act of boldness, Simon took Torey's hand and laced his fingers with hers. "It's definitely time."

She looked up at him with a tremulous smile. He returned her gaze, unable to look away. This was no place to speak of love. No place for him to take her into his arms, but the words of love passed silently between them, and the promise revealed in her eyes took away his breath.

A tug at his jacket caught his attention. He glanced down. Sarah gave him a heart-melting smile. "Miss Torey's not going to jail, is she?"

"No, Sweetie, she's not."

"Then can we pwease put the star on the twee?"

epilogue

Fluffy snow ushered in a beautiful Christmas morning. Torey looked out of her bedroom window and smiled at the winter wonderland.

With a contented sigh, she turned, walked to her wardrobe, and picked out her gown for the day. A lovely red, shirtwaist gown with a flowing skirt.

She sat at the vanity and pinned up her hair. Finally, she felt ready to join the festivities.

"Watch out!"

"Who left the front door open?"

Torey threw open her bedroom door and hurried to the steps. She looked down just in time to see Abe slipping and sliding on the foyer floor. He made a beeline for the living room.

"Get him before he knocks over the tree!" she called.

Crash!

"Oh, no, Abe!" The children's groans filled the room as Torey got there and found the tree knocked over, covering the presents. The dog had landed with a flop on the sofa, his muddy paws making new prints.

"I'm so sorry, Mrs. Crawford," Robert said. Despite the confusion, Torey noted how good it was to see him filling out and looking much more rested. It was a rare occasion for him to spend the day with his nieces and nephews.

Mrs. Crawford glared at the animal.

Katherine shook her head, clearly enraged. "That dog is a menace."

"He's pwetty." Sarah sat next to the massive St. Bernard

and placed her arm protectively around him. She received a wet lick for her effort. The animal sat, tongue hanging from his mouth, a huge red bow tied around his neck.

Mrs. Crawford's lips twitched. "Well, maybe not a menace exactly. And no harm was really done. See? The boys already have the tree back in place."

Minus a few ornaments, which Mrs. Crawford apparently opted not to mention.

"Well, he should be taken outside."

"I'm sure Frank will be here anytime to collect him."

Simon walked in wearing a sheepish grin. "Actually, Frank won't be coming to get ol' Abe. Merry Christmas, children. That animal is all yours."

Torey's heart nearly burst for love of this wonderful man.

A whoop went up from the children. "You mean it?" Mike asked. His newly found faith had made such a difference in his attitude that it was difficult to remember the angry boy he'd been only a few weeks ago.

Simon beamed, clearly as pleased at giving the dog to the children as they were to receive him. He nodded at Mike. "I mean it, Son."

"What's he doin' wearing a bow?" Toby demanded.

"Yeah," Tommy supported. "He ain't a girl."

Toby scowled and reached for the ribbon.

Sarah jumped in front of the dog. "No! He wooks pwetty."

"Boy dogs do not need to look pretty, Sarah!" Toby gave an exasperated sigh. "Mike, tell her! My dog ain't wearin' no bow!"

A smile lit Mike's face. "I think a Christmas present needs a bow. Leave her alone for now. Ol' Abe'll take it off when he's sick of it."

The twins wore identical expressions of disdain.

"Aw! Okay," Tommy said. "But this is the last one he's ever going to wear."

"Excuse me." Everyone turned at the sound of a timid voice at the doorway. "Th—the door was open."

"Ma!" The children scrambled to the slight woman. Tears spilled over as she tried to gather them into her arms all at once. "Oh, my darlings. How I've missed you."

"Miriam!" Robert jumped to his feet. Pure joy shone on his face. "You truly are alive."

Tears filled Torey's eyes, and she stared in amazement. The look on Simon's face revealed that Abe hadn't been his only present to the children. She went to him.

He smiled and slipped his arm about Torey's waist, pulling her against his side. "Merry Christmas," he murmured, his gaze flickering to her lips as though he'd very much like to kiss her.

Torey smiled. "How did you accomplish this?"

"I've had a detective on it since I discovered their mother wasn't dead after all. Robert truly thought she was dead. That's what his brother told him. The children just thought he was covering up for their father."

"Where has she been?"

"New York. That's where they lived before coming to Chicago. What the children never knew was that she didn't leave them. She ended up in the hospital after a beating by her husband. When she got out, her husband had taken the children and moved them here to be with Robert."

"However did they find her in New York?"

"I had a hunch, so I had the investigator check hospital records in New York. She had moved from the tenement building they had lived in, but he was able to track her through former neighbors she'd kept in contact with."

"You're wonderful, Simon Crawford." Torey beamed up at him.

"Come on." He grabbed her by the hand and glanced around. The reunion between mother and children was still going on in the doorway. With a scowl, he gave a frustrated breath and perused the room once more until his gaze finally lit on the slightly askew Christmas tree. He grinned and pulled her along until they were hidden behind its branches.

"Now," he said, pulling her into the circle of his arms. His head descended. "Merry Christmas."

"Merry Christmas." Her words were smothered as his lips covered hers in a heart-melting kiss. Torey molded against him, wrapping her arms tightly about his neck. When he finally broke the kiss, he kept her firmly grasped in his embrace. "I've been waiting until today to ask you this." He released her and dropped to one knee.

Torey's heart nearly beat from her chest, and tears filled her eyes as he presented her with a beautiful diamond ring.

"Oh, Simon."

He lifted his gaze to meet hers. "Will you marry me?"

"Abe! No!" Tommy's panicked voice ripped through the moment.

Torey screamed as the tree crashed away from them, leaving the entire room witness to Simon's proposal.

"Oh, praise the Lord," Mrs. Crawford breathed. Her eyes misted.

"What are you doin' on the floor?" Toby asked, his face etched in puzzlement.

"Don't you know nothin'?" Mike elbowed him.

"I know you're ugly!"

"Boys." Their mother's soft voice silenced them immediately.

"Sorry," they mumbled simultaneously.

Torey glanced down at Simon, who still held her hand. Exasperation clouded his face as he looked around the room.

"Yes," she said.

He looked back to her. "What?"

She pressed her palm against his cheek. "I said yes."

His eyes widened, and a slow grin spread across his lips.

He slipped the lovely token onto her ring finger and stood. Despite their audience, he pulled her into a bone-crushing embrace, lifting her off of her feet.

"What's going on?" Toby demanded.

"They're getting married," Melissa answered dreamily.

The twins groaned.

"Does this mean she ain't the maid no more?"

Torey smiled as Simon threw caution to the wind and drew her close once more.

She knew her days of cooking and cleaning were far from over, but from now on, she'd be doing those chores for her own family. And no life had ever looked more grand.

A Letter To Our Readers

Dear Reader:

    In order that we might better contribute to your reading enjoyment, we would appreciate your taking a few minutes to respond to the following questions. We welcome your comments and read each form and letter we receive. When completed, please return to the following:

Fiction Editor
Heartsong Presents
PO Box 719
Uhrichsville, Ohio 44683

1. Did you enjoy reading *Torey's Prayer* by Tracey V. Bateman?
  ❏ Very much! I would like to see more books by this author!
  ❏ Moderately. I would have enjoyed it more if

_____

_____

_____

2. Are you a member of **Heartsong Presents**? ❏ Yes ❏ No
  If no, where did you purchase this book? _____

_____

3. How would you rate, on a scale from 1 (poor) to 5 (superior), the cover design? _____

4. On a scale from 1 (poor) to 10 (superior), please rate the following elements.

____ Heroine	____ Plot
____ Hero	____ Inspirational theme
____ Setting	____ Secondary characters

5. These characters were special because?_____
_____
_____

6. How has this book inspired your life?_____
_____
_____

7. What settings would you like to see covered in future
   Heartsong Presents books? _____
_____
_____

8. What are some inspirational themes you would like to see
   treated in future books? _____
_____
_____

9. Would you be interested in reading other **Heartsong
   Presents** titles? ❑ Yes ❑ No

10. Please check your age range:
    ❑ Under 18   ❑ 18-24
    ❑ 25-34   ❑ 35-45
    ❑ 46-55   ❑ Over 55

Name_____
Occupation _____
Address _____
City_____ State_____ Zip_____

FRONTIER BRIDES

4 stories in 1

Four romances ride through the sagebrush of yesteryear by Colleen L. Reece.

Reece shares the compelling stories of people who put their lives on the line to develop a new land. . .and new love.

Historical, paperback, 464 pages, 5 $^3/_{16}$"x 8"

❤ • ❤ • ❤ • ❤ • ❤ • ❤ • ❤ • ❤ • ❤ • ❤ • ❤ • ❤

❤ • ❤ • ❤ • ❤ • ❤ • ❤ • ❤ • ❤ • ❤ • ❤ • ❤ • ❤

Presents

Great Inspirational Romance at a Great Price!

Heartsong Presents books are inspirational romances in contemporary and historical settings, designed to give you an enjoyable, spirit-lifting reading experience. You can choose wonderfully written titles from some of today's best authors like Peggy Darty, Sally Laity, Tracie Peterson, Colleen L. Reece, Debra White Smith, and many others.

When ordering quantities less than twelve, above titles are $2.97 each.
Not all titles may be available at time of order.

TRACEY V. BATEMAN lives in Missouri with her husband and their four children. She counts on her relationship with God to bring balance to her busy life. Grateful for God's many blessings, Tracey believes she is living proof that "all things are possible to them that believe," and she happily encourages anyone who will listen to dream big and see where God will take her.

Email address: tvbateman@aol.com
Website:www.traceyvictoriabateman.homestead.com/index.html

Books by Tracey V. Bateman

HEARTSONG PRESENTS
HP424—Darling Cassidy
HP468—Tarah's Lessons
HP524—Laney's Kiss
HP536—Emily's Place
HP555—But for Grace

Torey is determined to keep her secret from Simon, but he has other ideas.

"I appreciate your concern, Mr. Crawford, but I can't divulge more than you know for now."

His thumb caressed her arm. His gaze took in hers with an intensity that stole Torey's breath away. "Mr. Crawford, please. . ."

He took a step closer. "A moment ago you called me Simon."

"I—I did?"

Nodding, he reached forward and brushed back a strand of loose hair from her cheek. "You have lovely hair."

"Thank you, Mr. Crawford, but really. . ."

"Simon," he said softly, his gaze moving across her face and settling upon her lips.

"What?"

"I wish you'd call me Simon. Mr. Crawford sounds so formal."

"And proper." Torey drew herself up to her full height. Her knees felt like they might not hold her, and her insides quivered wildly, but she knew she had to draw a line. With a determination born of a desire to keep things properly balanced between them given their stations in life, she pulled her arm from his grasp.

"This isn't proper, Mr. Crawford."

"Maybe I want to court you. Would that be proper?" He didn't try to reach for her arm again; instead he leaned back against the doorframe.

Her heart slammed against her chest wall. "You want to court me?"

He nodded. "What do you think?"